Denita McDade is a passionate writer with a love for thrilling and fictional stories that stimulate the reader, and keep them craving for more. Using her vivid imagination, and wild and eccentric personality, she produced this compelling novel which is guaranteed to be readers' favorite.

Denita McDade

DISSEMBLANCE

AUSTIN MACAULEY PUBLISHERS™

LONDON · CAMBRIDGE · NEW YORK · SHARJAH

Ordering Information:
Quantity sales: special discounts are available on quantity purchases by corporations, associations, and others. For details, contact the publisher at the address below.

Publisher's Cataloging-in-Publication data
McDade, Denita
Dissemblance

ISBN 9781643781402 (Paperback)
ISBN 9781643781419 (Hardback)
ISBN 9781645366997 (ePub e-book)

Library of Congress Control Number: 2020901858

www.austinmacauley.com/us

First Published (2020)
Austin Macauley Publishers LLC
40 Wall Street, 28th Floor
New York, NY 10005
USA
mail-usa@austinmacauley.com
+1 (646) 5125767

Chapter I

Isaac, stared aimlessly out of the window as he crouched low in the passenger seat, while his brother drove down the winding road towards their house. The weather was cold, that fall afternoon and the auburn leaves painted the streets of the suburban neighborhood, where they lived with their parents. As they drove through the neighborhood, tears welled up in his eyes as he nervously slumped over, wallowing in the uncomfortable silence.

"You know, he is going to kill you," mumbled Mika under his breath, as he yanked the wheel, slowly turning into the driveway before screeching to a stop in front of the garage. He let out a sigh, as he examined Isaac across the car where he sulked quietly in his seat.

"I thought…I thought you promised, you were going to try to stay clean…" Mika continued to gripe with a disappointed look, as he shook his head shamefully.

Mika shut off the engine and began getting out of the car, to head inside the house, glancing quietly back at Isaac who remained motionless in the passenger seat, struggling to keep his composure.

"Look…I'll go in and talk to him for you, first. It'll lessen the blow a bit…" muttered Mika sympathetically, as he hesitantly pushed the door closed.

Mika, being the older of the two, always had a closer relationship with their father. He rarely got into trouble, growing up and after graduating college, returned home to work for his father, on his campaign and upcoming election.

"No! I'll do it," murmured Isaac softly, as he flung open the door and began to make his way up the driveway behind Mika, head hung low and dreading the confrontation that awaited him.

As he stiffly approached the house, the front door was abruptly thrown open and out stomped John, with an expression of scorn across his face.

"What the hell is wrong with you, boy?" he snarled viciously, as he glared down at him coldly, while Mika pushed past cautiously, making his way inside

The sound of his begrudging voice, echoed bitterly across the quiet suburban neighborhood and everyone within hearing distance, froze. Isaac fidgeted with his fingers, as he stared down at the flowerpots lining the porch, avoiding eye contact at all cost.

John, was a military man, as was his father before him and he was not lenient when it came to issues that could possibly jeopardize his political career. Mika made it a point from an early age, to fit in his father's mold, but Isaac was always the black sheep of the family.

"Dad, let me explain," blurted Isaac nervously, as he ran his hands through his hair, anxiously trying to think of an excuse. Before he could get another word out, John furiously retreated inside, slamming the door violently behind him.

Isaac flinched, startled by the loud crash of the door and he paused dumbfounded; while he pieced together, what had just happened. Seconds felt like hours, before he mustered up the courage to make his way inside the house. Turning the doorknob cautiously, he slipped inside, gently closing the door behind him. With knee's quavering, his eyes scanned the area for his father and he tiptoed silently inside. Once the coast was clear, he bolted across the room and climbed up the stairwell, toward his bedroom.

Mika smirked arrogantly, as he brushed past him. The former, was on his way back down the stairs.

"That was it? I would have smacked you around a bit at least," he snickered playfully, nudging Isaac as he walked past. Isaac grinned proudly as he spun him off, before closing his bedroom door swiftly and locking himself inside.

Later that evening, Nadia daintily knocked on the door and then cautiously twisted knob, slowly letting herself inside. "Honey, you didn't come down for dinner, so I brought you a sandwich," she whispered softly. She stepped over the mounds of dirty clothes carefully, gripping the plate tightly in her hand, while she made her way towards him.

Isaac slowly poked his head out from under the sheets, lazily ripping the covers off him. He sat upright, rubbing his eyes tiredly. Nadia, stumbled through the dank room and set the plate gently down on his nightstand. Calming down, she sat beside him placing her hand comfortingly on his back.

"I know, your father's upset, but just give him a few days and he will calm down," she said tenderly, as she leaned and kissed him on his forehead. "If you need anything, I will be downstairs sweetie," she continued, as she patted him gently on his back. Slowly, she pulled herself up from the crumpled sheets and shuffled through the clutter back out to the hallway. "Goodnight, Zacky," she whispered quietly, as she pulled the bedroom door closed and disappeared into the darkness.

Chapter II

As the sun poked through the blinds early the next morning, Isaac rolled sluggishly from his bed and headed downstairs to the kitchen, to fix something to eat. One of the many rules in the house, was that everyone was out of bed by 7:00 am and if you weren't going to school or working, then you were stuck handing out flyers for the campaign. That, was the last thing he wanted to do all weekend.

A few months earlier, Isaac had taken a job in marketing for his dad's campaign, but was quickly released from his role after a neighbor caught him smoking marijuana, while setting up displays. John, being the predominant local politician, had to pay a lot of money to make that incident disappear; which undeniably became the last time that Isaac ever mixed work, with play.

As he moseyed into the kitchen, he abruptly stopped at the sight of John, who was reading the daily newspaper quietly, at the head of the table. Timidly, he approached the table pulling out a chair from across his father and nervously sitting down, as he stared at the plate in front of him.

"Don't make any plans, you're not going anywhere today," angrily erupted John under his breath, as he peered over the newspaper looking towards him.

"Yes sir," he mumbled dolefully in reply, as he slouched low in his chair, sighing morosely under his breath, as he fiddled with the fork in front of him. Jail time sounded better, than spending a Saturday hanging around the house, stuck and catering to his demanding father.

Shortly, after Nadia had served breakfast, the ringing doorbell echoed throughout the house, prompting John to quickly rush over to the front door and swing it open without delay. Isaac listened quietly, as he heard him welcome the company politely, seating them in the living room.

"Isaac, come on in here, there are some people I'd like to introduce you to," he called heartily from the other room, which was followed by the sound of small talk.

Isaac rolled his eyes, lazily pushing himself up from the table. He dropped his plate into the soapy sink and shuffled past his mother, on the way to the living room. He curiously poked his head around the corner and glared at the two older sharply dressed men perched on the couch, while they waited for him impatiently.

Isaac strolled warily into the room, as they rose to their feet, acknowledging him with shrewd grins across their faces.

"Isaac, my man! I'm Bill, this is my colleague Alan, and we're with the Movement Foundation," muttered Bill excitedly, as he approached Isaac, extending his hand. Hesitantly, he observed the men up and down, while cautiously greeting them with a hesitant handshake.

"Come, take a seat," called John from across the room, as he gestured to him while he rocked comfortably in his recliner.

Isaac inhaled deeply and stiffly made his way toward the couch, where he sat uneasily across from the men.

"I've been a proud supporter of the Foundation for many years," said his father. "The Foundation, has been very close to my heart and it's the one that truly benefits from my campaign and the people of this fair town. As the upcoming election is upon us, I think it'd be a good time, for you to join the Foundation and seize this great opportunity!" Rambled his father boastfully, as he gazed across at him. "They, have been kind enough to extend a scholarship for you, to join their next outing this coming summer," he continued, with a proud grin plastered across his face.

"A scholarship?" replied Isaac, as he shook his head pessimistically. "My grades are shit, I smoke weed; why would they choose me, for a scholarship? Shouldn't you be giving these to, I don't know, some nerds, or something?" he chuckled under his breath, as he slouched back into the cushions.

"It was actually, an easy decision for us to make! John here, has been telling us some great things and you are exactly the kind of candidate, we have been looking for," Alan quickly pointed out, as he leaned convincingly toward him.

"So, what exactly would I be joining here? Some type of stupid religious cult, or political group?" questioned Isaac, as he ran his hands loosely through his hair, baffled by the offer. "'Cause, if that's the case. I pass."

13

"You, will be joining a group of elite men such as yourself, who were hand-picked to make a difference. Some might even call it, an offering of sorts," Alan responded haughtily, as he locked eyes with John, gleaming with a catty smirk on his face.

"Look, Son! This, is an opportunity of a lifetime. These men, have been nice enough to provide us with this scholarship and it's crucial you consider it, on behalf of my campaign," firmly interrupted John, as he adjusted the collar on his shirt, peering belligerently across at him.

"I'm supposed to just give up my summer plans, to do some fucking expedition to God knows where, so your CAMPAIGN looks good? Not fucking happening," responded Isaac furiously as he sat up on the sofa, rolling up his sleeves in frustration.

"Watch, your goddamn mouth, this is not a discussion. In three weeks after graduation, you will be going! You blew off college, you won't keep a job, and your friends are a bunch of junkies. No son of mine, lives under my roof and embarrasses me in that manner," John roared across the room aggressively, as he stood up from the recliner, in confrontation.

Isaac, jumped up from his seat and stormed past the men wildly; their eyes were focused intently on him, while he made his way to the stairs. As he charged angrily up the stairs, a piece of décor was knocked down from the wall. He cursed under his breath, all the way to his bedroom, violently slamming the door behind him.

John breathed in heavily, as he pressed out the wrinkles on his dress shirt and adjusted his collar, before gradually settling back into his seat, as he regained composure. The house was still, as Nadia slowly made her way from the kitchen into the living room, placing her hand on his shoulder in support.

"That, went better than I expected. We'll be in touch," murmured Alan, as he picked himself up from the couch and made his way toward the front door, with Bill in tow. Nadia hurried past the men into the foyer, pulling open the front door to let them out. Bill turned toward John, tipping his hat with a slight nod, before they disappeared down the walkway.

Chapter III

That evening, Mika sluggishly trudged to the house from the office. Hanging up his jacket, he entered tiredly, making a quick detour to the kitchen. He cautiously squeezed past his mother, giving her a peck on the cheek as she cooked dinner and then made his way up the stairs, to his bedroom.

He sneered, as he shuffled past Isaacs's bedroom door, lugging his heavy briefcase while he slowly loosened his tie. "Lazy little shit," he grunted under his breath, before tossing his things on the bed and heading out into the hall, towards Isaac's door.

"Open up, asshole, it's me," he grumbled irritably, banging against the door. "You better not be asleep, jerk," he continued to ramble, while pushing the door open and letting himself in. The room, was empty and lights were off. A chilly draft coming in from the cracked window, blew the curtains. Mika sighed with irritation, as he staggered over to the window, pulling it closed, as he had done on so many nights before. Once again, Isaac had sneaked out and Mika knew exactly where he was.

Miles away, in an empty field known to the locals as Derby Point, Isaac and his girlfriend, Michelle, lay under the stars, in the back of her father's rusty, old, pick-up truck.

Earlier that evening, Michelle stole the keys to the truck and then climbed out of her bedroom window, while her father slept in a drunken stupor, as he did most nights. Escaping to Derby Point with Isaac, was a refuge from the stress and abuse she regularly endured at home.

Michelle, lived alone with her father Odis, in a small town, about fifteen minutes outside the city. Her mother had died of cancer, when she was still in grade school and Odis's drinking had spiraled out of control. He worked as a local handyman, bringing in just enough money to keep the house from foreclosure and for food on the table, but most nights he was despondent and in an inebriated rage.

Tonight though, it was Isaac who was in need of refuge, as Michelle curled up in his arms as a crisp breeze blew through her curly hair.

"So, are you going?" she mumbled daintily, as their limbs intertwined on the cold steel, twirling a clump of her hair anxiously, at the thought of him leaving her for the entire summer.

Isaac sighed dejectedly, as he squeezed her tightly to himself, kissing her gently on the top of her forehead.

"What choice, do I have? I'm tired of running, tired of disappointing him. Maybe, this will prove something finally," he replied earnestly, while loosening his hold around her and slowly propping himself up, hunching over in contemplation.

Gradually he turned, peering back over his shoulder, watching dolefully as she dabbed at the tears rolling down her cheek, from the corner of her eyes. Isaac cracked a grin, as he reached down and gently wiped her face and looked intently into her eyes. "You're always saying you need a break from me, well here you go!" He murmured playfully, as he gave her a jovial wink.

Michelle pushed him away, as she rolled her eyes. "This is not funny Isaac, why do you have to go? What about our plans? What about me?" she blurted wistfully, as her voice trembled and her eyes welled with tears.

"Come on babe, give me a break, please! Okay, so what? I stay and we live at your pop's house, struggling to make ends meet our whole lives? This, might be a good opportunity for me. For us!" he replied defensively, as he chipped at the cracks in the old paint with frustration.

"Chelly! It's not that I want to leave you, but I need to do this. God knows, I don't want to end up like your fath...er... I'm sorry," he continued meekly, before hanging his head low in anguish.

Michelle exhaled loudly, as she pushed herself up beside him, wrapping her arms tightly around his shoulders. She slowly leaned and kissed him reassuringly on his cheek, as he hung his head remorsefully.

"It's okay," she mumbled, before kissing him gingerly on the side of his face and giving him a forgiving smile.

They embraced each other and they both knew, what was to happen at that very moment! Isaac would be going away for the summer, in just three short weeks after his graduation.

Dawn was approaching, when Michelle dropped Isaac off, a few streets from his house, staying out of sight from his neighborhood. Isaac knew, he wouldn't hear the end of it for sneaking out and the last thing he wanted anyone to see, was who he was with. John never warmed up to Michelle, not over anything that she had done, but merely for the fact that she came from an impoverished family and he didn't want his boys associating with the lower class.

Isaac shivered, as he hopped down from the idling pick-up onto the cold pavement, slamming the steel door behind him. He gave a slight wave, before jamming his hands into his pockets for warmth. He then began to walk quickly up the foggy street, towards his house. Springtime, in the mountains wasn't always flowers and sunshine, the mornings were cold with icy dew on the grass, and clouds darkened the roads.

As he neared the house, he jogged to the side gate, left propped open and made his way around to the back yard and over to the old oak tree, which grew outside his window. Abruptly, he came to a startling halt. He saw Mika standing there, rubbing the sleep from his eyes, and leaning against the tree, as he tightened the belt on his robe.

"You know, you really ought to start switching up on your routine," he yawned out loudly, as he cracked a swaggering smile.

Isaac, rolled his eyes and cursed under his breath, as he stomped toward him, in confrontation.

"Spare me your bullshit, Mika! I don't need this right now. Just go on ahead and tell Dad like you always do," he groaned bitterly, as he roughly brushed past him, knocking into his shoulder.

"Whoa, whoa, calm down. I just want to talk," pleaded Mika, as he raised his hands defensively, following behind Isaac till he gradually slowed and turned towards him, with a scowl on his face.

Mika, approached him and gently placed his arm around Isaac's shoulder and peered sympathetically into his eyes.

"I just wanted to say, that I didn't know anything about this and I'm sorry they're making you go. I tried to talk to him, but he wasn't having any of it. I know how close you and Michelle are, and…" he began to stutter, struggling to say the right thing to diffuse the tension.

Isaac let out a deep sigh, welcoming his brother's appeal to reason as he relaxed and loosened his rigid stance.

"Hey, if the ol' man wants me to go, I'll go. At least I'll get a break, from your square ass for a while," he shot back with a caustic sneer, snickering under his breath.

Lunging forward unexpectedly, Mika clasped his arm tightly around Isaac's neck and held him firmly in a headlock.

"Ha! How about you quit sneaking out, you little shit and don't forget this square and can take you down, any day!" he shouted playfully, before heaving him to the ground. They wrestled, as the sun began to rise over the hills.

Chapter IV

The house was in disarray the following weeks leading up the graduation, as the family chaotically prepared for his departure. John, met with members of the foundation often, getting all the proper authorizations and documents required for Isaac's travel in order, as Isaac, wasn't yet a legal adult and needed his guardian's permission.

Isaac cringed, as he was hauled back and forth to the family physicians for routine physical checks and other necessary immunizations; to be certified as fit to travel, according to the Foundation's strict regulations. His anxiety grew, as he counted down the days prior to his leaving, wondering what to expect and most importantly, nervous over how things would be different, once he returned.

The weekend preceding his graduation started out like any other, as Isaac sluggishly got out of bed, making his way slowly downstairs for breakfast. As he drifted toward the kitchen, rubbing the sleep from his eyes, he noticed his father's office door closed, with the light on inside.

Curious about this, he pulled out a chair from the kitchen table and sat adjacent to the room. He reached across the table, for the box of cereal and watched the door, distractedly filling the bowl in front of him to the brim. He ate quietly, as he watched his mother discreetly enter and then exit the office, quickly closing the door behind her.

As she walked back toward the kitchen, Isaac tapped her arm lightly, grabbing her attention, while he continued to peer at the closed door.

"What's going on in there?" he whispered hoarsely under his breath, looking strangely at the door across the room.

Nadia smiled nonchalantly, as she patted him on the top of his head and continuing past him to the kitchen.

"Oh, your father is just tying up some last-minute loose ends, with your upcoming trip, honey," she replied airily, while moving over to the sink and turning on the faucet, to drown out any further conversation.

Isaac grunted uneasily in response and scratched his head, puzzled by the goings on, before rising from the table and excusing himself, to get back upstairs to his room.

Later that afternoon, he heard the doorbell echo throughout the house, prompting him to peek curiously down, towards the front of the house. His eyes widened, as they rested on a black Cadillac parked out front, with the license plate reading "MVFNDTN."

Isaac smirked, before quickly hurtling downstairs and eagerly swinging open the front door to greet them, but before he could get a word out, Alan firmly pushed him aside and advanced into the house demanding to speak to John, with Bill trailing behind him.

Isaac staggered out of the way in dismay, as they aggressively passed by, muttering under their breaths; striding across the living room, towards John's office. Bill, began to pound impatiently against the door, until it was flung open and the men filed into the office and slammed it shut behind them.

Isaac's jaw dropped, as he closed the front door apprehensively, then sat down on the couch observing and listening to the grim commotion coming from the other room. Whatever was going on in there, involved him and his newfound organization.

Hours later, Mika returned home from the office and immediately noticed Isaac slouched over on the couch, in the empty, dark living room. Mika slipped off his jacket, folding it delicately over his forearm, as he glanced over at Isaac sitting motionless on the couch, staring attentively at the door of their father's office.

"Who's in there with him?" he questioned softly, as he continued on through the living room, coming to a stop in front of Isaac, as he focused on the door.

"Those two idiots from the Foundation, but something isn't right…" Isaac replied uneasily, followed by an exasperated yawn. "They barged in here, pissed off about something and they've been in there for hours," he continued, as he sat upright and stretched, rubbing his tired eyes.

Isaac, pushed himself up from the couch and began to stumble across the room towards the kitchen, followed by Mika.

"Fuck! I'm starving," he groaned aloud, before pausing restlessly in front of his father's office and leaning in closely, pressing his ear to the door. Mika smirked, as he nudged him in his back, pushing him past the door and into the kitchen.

"Just chill out. It's probably something about insurance, or something stupid. I heard him on the phone, arguing with someone about that earlier. Now, quit worrying!" he said convincingly, as he guided Isaac to one of the chairs, plopping him down into it near the table.

Isaac, let out a deep sigh as he slouched back in his chair lazily, "You say that shit, 'cause you're not the one getting shipped out, to God knows where. I need to know, what is going on," he said apprehensively, as he glared glassy eyed over at his brother, watching him dig through the refrigerator.

Mika smiled, as he pulled out the lunchmeat and plunked it down onto the counter, while kicking the refrigerator door closed. "Okay, okay! I'll talk to him tomorrow and figure out what's going on," he reassured Isaac, as he looked back over his shoulder and said sincerely, "I promise."

Chapter V

On the evening of the graduation, Isaac napped upstairs in his room. When he faintly heard his name echo, from the bottom of the stairwell in the distance, he called out hoarsely, "I'm up...I'm up," and he fumbled his way out from the bed sheets, scanning the cluttered floor for something clean to wear.

He dressed quickly, stopping by the hall bathroom to splash cold water on his face and slick his untamed hair back from out of his eyes. "It's show time," he muttered under his breath, as he checked his appearance once more and then shut off the light, hurrying towards the stairs.

"I told you, we were leaving this house by 7:00 pm. You aren't even on time, when it's your ass on the line," bellowed John from the living room, as he watched him descend the stairs leisurely.

Isaac, let out a gasp as he grazed past him, plopping down unhurriedly on a chair at the kitchen table, glancing around for something to eat.

"Would you like me to make you a sandwich, sweetie?" Nadia called out over her shoulder, as she plunged her hands into the sink full of soapy water, washing the dirty dishes left over from dinner.

"No, we don't have time," John hollered crossly from the next room, before Isaac had a chance to respond. "I'll be waiting in the truck," he continued to bluster, while trudging across the living room toward the front door and slamming it behind him.

Isaac pushed himself up from the table bitterly, snatching an apple from the fruit bowl. He sulked, while exiting the kitchen. "Thanks anyway, Mom," he mumbled over his shoulder, as he picked up the pace, hurrying outside and over to the truck.

The engine roared, as John accelerated down the dark street, meticulously avoiding eye contact with Isaac, as he glanced occasionally in the rear-view mirror.

As they approached the high school, John began to clear his throat nervously, glancing apprehensively back at Isaac, while he adjusted the collar of his dress shirt.

"You know, I..." John began to growl, hesitating, as he coughed uncomfortably, "You know I love...I mean everything I do, it's for a purpose. For the good of this family and I...I just wanted you to know that," he continued solemnly, as he gradually veered into the school parking lot, stopping in front of the auditorium.

Isaac sat quietly in the back seat, nodding conspicuously then began to slowly exit the truck, thrusting at the door to close behind him. He quickly jogged up the concrete stairs leading towards the entrance, glancing back over his shoulder, as the truck screeched off and out into the distance.

Later that evening as the graduation commenced, Isaac scanned through the rows of benches full of supporters, until he spotted his father along with his media team, who had their cameras rolling. "I figured as much," he sighed under his breath, while nervously inching his way in the line, to get closer to the stage.

Unlike his brother, he hated the attention given to him for being a politician's son and anxiously avoided it, at all costs. As he heard his name echo over the loud speaker, he shyly shuffled past the other students, while they patted him encouragingly on the back in recognition of his status. A spotlight glared upon him and the loud roar from the audience drowned out the announcer, as he timidly walked to the center of the stage, to receive his diploma. He managed a smile, as he squinted from the bright light, peering out once again at the sea of spectators, this time noticing faces from his Father's Foundation seated discreetly on the benches, with sober expressions on their faces as they looked on.

Isaac, kept his eye on them as he shuffled in line to his seat, alongside the last of the graduating students, while the principal made his closing remarks. Within seconds, the auditorium erupted in applause, followed by dozens of caps being tossed into the air, as the student's celebrated the occasion.

As the crowd settled, he noticed that the men had vanished in the commotion, exiting the building without a trace. Isaac skimmed attentively through the mass of people, but was thrown off guard, as Michelle approached him passionately, jumping into his arms.

"We did it, babe! We finally did it," she squealed hysterically, while clasping her arms tightly around his neck and blocking his view. Isaac let out a frustrated gasp, as he slowly wrapped his arms around her in return, kissing her distractedly on the forehead.

"Yea, we did it," he uttered uncaringly, while holding her loosely, still attempting to survey the cluster of people surrounding them.

Soon after they embraced, Michelle jerked impulsively, making her loosen her hold around him and she reluctantly pulled away.

"Daddy?" she whispered under her breath, nervously pushing away and making her way towards Otis, through the packed crowd.

Otis stood dazed in the distance, disoriented by the flurry of people around him. Michelle, wedged her way through the flood of people and rushed toward him. When he spotted her in the crowd, he broke into a toothless grin, waving his hands drunkenly in the air.

"I didn't think you'd make it," blurted out Michelle, as tears welled in her eyes and she cautiously approached him, holding her arms out.

"I wouldn't have missed it for the world," he zealously replied, smelling of old gin, as he pulled her into a tight hug.

Isaac smiled, as he watched from across the room, slowly drifting towards them.

"I'm glad you could make it, Mr. Gallows," he said whimsically with a cheerful grin, as he gave him a sturdy pat on the shoulder.

Otis released his grip on Michelle, as he brusquely turned toward Isaac, grabbing hold of him with a smile on his face.

"Get over here, kid," he bellowed jovially, hiccupping between words and all the while struggling to keep from toppling over, as he leaned on Isaac for support.

"Okay…okay, let's get you home, sir," he chuckled in response, holding onto his arm, and hoisting him up, as they shuffled their way towards the exit through the thinning crowd.

As Isaac supported Otis out to the parking lot, Michelle followed behind embarrassed, through the dispersing the crowd, hanging her head low.

Mika, caught a glimpse of them from across the parking lot and began moving towards them slowly, animatedly clapping his hands.

"I thought I'd never see the day," he blurted out jokingly, followed by a comical wink, as he grabbed hold of Otis's other arm, helping to carry him along the sidewalk.

"So, how long did he stay sober this time?" Mika murmured faintly under his breath, as Michelle trailed shamefully behind, avoiding eye contact with the curious spectators. Isaac scowled, as he shook his head disgracefully, while walking quickly through the parking lot.

"Well, if it makes you feel better…Dad came and he was very proud of you," Mika continued, as they shuffled their way over to Otis's truck, propping him on the passenger seat.

"Ha, you think it's because he cares? It's for publicity," scoffed Isaac, while looking out for John out of the corner of his eye. "Mayor's son graduates and goes on a mission trip. Front page of the Chronical," he continued, impersonating his father, and followed it by a quiet chuckle, as he rolled his eyes.

Mika grinned, giving him a playful nudge, before turning and starting towards his car, in in the dimly lit lot. "I truly think he is starting to come around, or at least he is trying to," he yelled out convincingly over his shoulder, as he went. "Come, ride with me, little bro, I want to talk to you," he continued to holler, before receding from sight and going to his car parked across the lot.

"I better get him home, anyway," whispered Michelle, before cracking a forced smile and urging him to go with Mika. "I'll be all right, I promise. See you later?" she asked, hopefully looking at him, while making her way around to the driver's seat of the truck.

Isaac stood thoughtfully, as he watched the truck disappear down the street, just as Mika shouted out from across the lot, again.

"Let's go," he bellowed, from the driver's side of his BMW, prompting Isaac to bolt across the parking lot, towards him.

As he settled in his seat, Mika drove out of the parking lot and onto the main road, with the windows down and the music blaring. He could feel the tension, as he periodically glanced across at Isaac, who stared silently out of the window at the passing cars.

Quietly, he reached down, lowering the volume of the stereo and cleared his throat, to draw Isaacs's attention. "So, uh! I saw a few of those guys from that Foundation, there tonight. They seemed like good folks, huh?" he blurted out nonchalantly, breaking the silence, as glanced over in Isaac's direction with a smug expression.

Isaac shrugged indifferently, as he continued to stare uninterestedly out of the window.

"I mean, supporting your graduation, offering you a scholarship...I gotta say, that is pretty awesome," he continued, rambling off optimistically, hoping to lighten the mood.

"Look Mika, I know what you are trying to do and it won't work. Something is wrong, with those people and I just can't put my finger on it yet," Isaac said sullenly, crossing his arms in defense, as they continued down the street.

"Come on man... You won't even give the man a try? Lighten up!" Exclaimed Mika, as he threw up his arms in frustration, causing the car to swerve. "Look, if anything is going on, I will hold myself responsible, okay? Hell! I'll even confront the old man...with my fists," he continued humorously, as he reached out, punching Isaac heartily on his shoulder.

Isaac's stiff demeanor loosened, as he eased back in his seat chuckling under his breath, then letting out a comforting sigh while nodding his head. "Okay, big bro, I'm trusting you," he mumbled reluctantly, then leaned back comfortably in his seat, as they drove the rest of the way home.

Chapter VI

Later that night Isaac struggled to sleep, as the gleam of the moon shone through the corner of the blinds and into his eyes. He peered over at the clock beside his bed, focusing on the time, then let out an agonizing moan as he rolled over plonking his face firmly into his pillow, to block the light.

Just as he began to nod off, he was jolted awake by the notification tone on his cell phone, across the room. Isaac groaned with exhaustion, as he pushed himself up and stumbled across the dank room, to check the message.

He yawned, wiping the crust from the corner of his eyes, as he focused on the blurry screen in front of him. 'Come outside,' it said.

"About damn time," he croaked breathlessly, as he padded over to the window, gazing down at Otis's truck parked along the curb in the cold night. Quickly, he threw on some shoes, grabbed his jacket off the floor and tiptoed out of his bedroom and out into the dark hallway.

As he crept past his parent's room, he couldn't help but overhear a murmur coming through the door, which was open just a crack. Curiously he inched his way closer, pressing his ear against the door and heard the soft whimper from his mother who was crying, followed by the muffled and stern words of his father.

"Nadia, we've been over this. It's for the best," he said roughly.

"I'm just…I'm just going to miss him," she responded hesitantly, in a soft whisper between sniffles and then continued to weep silently.

Isaac grimaced, moved by her heartache over his leaving. He stepped back quietly from the door and went down the stairs. Stealthily, he darted through the house and out of the front door, sprinting at full speed down the gloomy street toward Michelle, who sat in the truck looking out for him.

As he came up to the back of the truck, he hoisted himself onto the bed of the pickup. Michelle, shifted the truck into gear, revving the engine as she veered down the road and headed to Derby Point.

Once there, she swiftly maneuvered the truck to a ledge facing the city's skyline, as the sun began to creep up slowly behind the buildings in the distance. Impatiently, she shut off the engine, thrusting open the door and making her way around to the back of the truck, where Isaac awaited.

She smiled mischievously, as she climbed over the back rail, inching her way passionately on top of him, as he lay sprawled out with his arms folded under his head, gazing calmly up at the fading stars.

She rested her head tenderly on his chest, as he gazed down at her, running his fingers through her hair in admiration. Isaac smelt the flowery aroma from her hair, as he kissed her passionately on top of her forehead. He lifted her chin up from his chest, as he gazed lovingly into her eyes. Then he slowly pulled her towards him kissing her sensually, as he gradually slid his hand down her torso, caressing every single curve.

Time stood still, as they made love in the back of the old pickup, savoring the little time they had together, with a million thoughts rambling through their minds.

"Babe, I can't stay. I have to get home now," he gloomily whispered, as he held her tightly in his arms. By now, the sun was up and the sound of birds chirping filled the air and echoed across the field.

"I know," she quietly replied, her voice trembling and holding back her tears. Isaac let out a deep sigh, as he raised her gently off his chest and tossed her the blouse which was lying crumpled next to him. He fumbled around for his jeans, all the while shielding himself from the eyes of the morning joggers, as they passed by in the distance.

As he leaped from the back of truck, he let out an exhausted yawn, before turning and hoisting her gently down onto the grass beside him. Isaac grabbed hold of her and walked her over to the passenger side of the truck, where he pushed her up into the cab slamming the door, before making his way around to the driver's side.

The ride home was wistful, as Michelle slouched over, resting her head glumly against his shoulder as he drove. They passed through the familiar neighborhood, going towards his house and the muffled sound of her whimper grew louder, as she wiped away the warm tears streaming down her cheeks with her sleeve.

"Please don't go," she blurted out hysterically, as they veered down the street, leading towards his house. Isaac sat motionless, eyes glazed over with tears, as he drifted to the side of the road a few blocks up from his house, slowing to a complete stop.

"Fuck, Michelle, you know I have to go. Don't do this to me, please," he complained, as he unfastened his seatbelt, staring out of the window. "I'll only be gone a few months and when I get back, I'll get you the hell out of here. I promise," he continued, turning towards her reassuringly as he wiped her tear stained cheeks.

Isaac got off the truck and Michelle slid over the passenger seat. He then leaned in through the open window for one last kiss, before making his way up the winding road, towards his house. Moments later, he heard Michelle's restless voice call from behind.

"Wait," she screamed, waving her arm desperately in the air. Quickly, she left the truck, running towards him as she anxiously unfastened the clasp of the gold bracelet she wore, which was given to her, by her grandfather. Michelle grabbed hold of Isaacs's arm and clamped the bracelet around his wrist, as she lovingly looked up at him.

Isaac smiled as he grabbed hold of her, pulling her towards him passionately. "I'll never take it off, I promise," he said devotedly, before releasing his grip on her and continued on his way to the house.

Michelle watched him walk away for a few seconds; then gloomily shuffled back to the truck. Starting the engine, she morosely began her journey back home.

When Isaac heard the engine flare, he turned toward the sound, standing motionless in the middle of the street. He watched, as the love of his life sped away down the road, kicking up dust and whispered, "Bye, Michelle!"

Chapter VII

As Isaac approached the house and made his way in, the sweet smell of homemade waffles filled the air. He crept quietly across the living room, hoping not to be seen.

"Isaac, there you are! Where have you been honey?" called out his mother enthusiastically from the kitchen, as she poked her head out from around the corner.

"Come on in here and eat darling, I made your favorite blueberry waffles with scrambled eggs," she continued, as she came towards him, pulling him gently by the wrist over to the kitchen table. Isaac hesitated, looking around the room for his father, as he shuffled behind her and plopped down on a chair. Famished as he was, he immediately reached across the table grabbing a stack of waffles off the serving tray, while his stomach growled.

"Where's everybody?" mumbled Isaac, in between bites, as his eyes scanned the empty house.

"Mika and your father left a while ago," she answered, as she wiped down the counters with a dishtowel. "Everyone is out looking for you sweetie. You really had us all worried," she continued, draping the towel on the edge of the sink, as she looked over her shoulder at him uneasily.

As he had finished eating, he began to get up to clear his plate from the table, when a boisterous knock on the door, echoed throughout the house.

"I'll get it!" Nadia shouted, as she quickly wiped her hands on her apron, before darting towards the front door.

Isaac eased back into his chair, listening to the whispers coming from the other room, as his mother spoke through the slightly opened door, very discreetly.

Moments later, the door slammed abruptly and Nadia casually wandered back into the kitchen, straightening her apron as she resumed drying the dishes.

"Who was that?" asked Isaac, as he saw her behaving casually, with no explanation offered.

"Oh, that was no one important. Hurry, go get yourself ready though. Your father will be here shortly, to pick you up," she cut him off, immediately changing the subject as she urged him to get up from the table.

Isaac grunted, as he dropped his plate into the sink and hurried past, planting a kiss on his mother's cheek on his way out of the kitchen. "Food was great, thanks Mom," he said graciously and quickly retreated to his room.

Isaac, closed the door to his room and locked it behind him. He then shuffled through the rummage scattered on the floor and over to the window. He reached through the tattered blinds, tugging open the window, to let in the dewy morning breeze to air out the room.

Casually, he walked over to his alarm clock, fumbling around with the knob until the radio started blaring. Bobbing his head to the music, he reached up to the top shelf of his closet, gently lowering down the old shoebox he kept there.

He tore off the frayed lid, as he carried it to his bed and sifted through the old baseball cards and junk inside, until he stumbled across an old cigarette box stashed at the bottom. He carefully dug into the box, latching onto the plastic bag full of pot and grinned as he opened it, inhaling its pungent aroma as he sat down on his bed.

Isaac reached for his pipe and lighter hidden under his mattress and quickly stuffed it full of pot, as he'd done many times before. As he lit the pipe, he closed his eyes and slowly lay back, zoning out while the music played in the background.

Just as he began to slip into a lethargic daze, he heard a muffled thud against the bedroom door over the loud booming music. Isaac propped himself up, as he used his thumb to snuff out the burning ember, left in the pipe. He then quickly stuffed it back under mattress.

"Comin'…" he grunted hoarsely, coughing, as he fanned at the lingering cloud of smoke. He apprehensively opened the door just a crack and peered anxiously out into the hallway, rubbing his hazy eyes.

"It's just me," barked Mika between coughs, as he gagged from the smoke that emanated from the room. "Really! In the house? Get your ass up, turn this shit off and do something about the smell," he continued bitterly, before turning and making his way back downstairs.

Isaac, rolled his eyes while he closed his door, then stumbled back over to his radio yanking out the power cord and abruptly shutting off the music. He grabbed the cologne sitting on top of his dresser and began to spray himself repeatedly, hoping to disguise any remnants of the pot, just as the familiar sound of the garage door opening, shook the house.

Isaac gulped nervously, as he glanced out of the window down at the driveway as his father's truck slowly rolled in. He noticed that Bill and Alan were along with him, as the truck came to a halt and they got out of the vehicle.

"Here we go," he mumbled with irritation, grabbing hold of the large suitcase that his mother had packed for him a few days earlier and began to drag it behind him, out into hallway. As he hoisted it down the stairs, John entered the house and without a word grasped the handle, yanking it form his grip and dragging it out to the truck.

Isaac, strolled out behind him and down the walkway towards his father's truck, making his way to the cab as John wrestled around with the suitcase, loading it into the trunk. Quickly he climbed inside, peeking over his shoulder as he surveyed the trunk.

"Packing kind of light, aren't you, guys?" Isaac blurted sarcastically, while tugging on his seatbelt, clasping it secure. Alan, who was seated across from him cracked a sly smile, as John glanced up silently and slammed the trunk door closed, ignoring his comment.

"We need to hit the highway, if we want to make good time," he growled sternly, as he climbed into truck, tapping on the horn to grab everyone's attention.

Seconds later, Nadia peeked out through the blinds then came running out of the house with Mika in tow, signaling them to wait, as they rushed towards the truck.

"I love you. I…I… Just take care of yourself the best you can, okay?" she called out, as she made her way briskly around to Isaac's side of the truck. Isaac cracked an adoring smile, while he rolled down the window, gazing across at her bloodshot eyes that she dabbed erratically, as the tears were streaming from her eyes. Gently he reached out, wiping away the makeup stains on her face and leaned through the window, kissing her on her cheek.

"It's only a few months, Mom. Stop crying, I'll be home soon," he said, as he lifted her chin, grinning at her.

Nadia forced a watery smile, as she tousled his hair playfully then glanced over at John, who was watching her through the rear-view mirror.

"That's my brave boy," she said cautiously, and hesitantly turned away, moving slowly back up the walkway toward the house, as Mika came towards the truck, giving her a comforting squeeze on the shoulder as he passed by her.

Immediately, he started chuckling under his breath, while he shook his head from side to side, jovially approaching the window. "I'm not gonna cry over you leaving, but can I get a hug at least?" he said, as he leaned in wrapping his arms around Isaac. Isaac laughed, as he sat enveloped in his hug, while Mika let out a loud and comforting groan. "Take care, little brother," he continued to mutter, as he patted him vigorously on his back.

"Okay, okay, you won't miss me that much," replied Isaac, as he slowly pushed him off, with a caustic grin across his face. Mika smirked, loosened his grip, and backed away from the truck, as John shifted into gear and began to slowly reverse out of the driveway, rolling toward the main street.

As they veered sharply onto the road, Mika briskly jogged behind waving his arms animatedly in the air to grab

Isaacs's attention. "I'm so proud of you, brother," he hollered at the top of his lungs as the truck accelerated up the road, disappearing over the hill and out of sight.

Chapter VIII

Isaac, sat quietly in the back seat, staring absent-mindedly out of the window for most of the way on the drive to the airport, as John and the others remained drawn back and focused on the road.

"So, uh, when we get there, wherever that is, do I get time to explore around or how does this work?" asked Isaac, as he nervously fidgeted with his fingers, glancing around at them inquisitively. Alan, let out a caustic snicker under his breath and gaped at him through the rear-view mirror, taken aback by his question.

"When we get there?" Crassly responded Alan. "No, Son, we aren't going anywhere, you're making this journey alone," he said quietly, while staring thoughtfully out of the window at the desolate terrain.

Isaac slouched back his seat dumbfounded, as he pondered over what exactly he had gotten himself into, by agreeing to the trip. "Just relax, everything is going to go smoothly," reassured his Father in a sober tone, as he reached down to turn up the volume on the radio, drowning out any further conversation.

Isaac shook his head in dismay, as he closed his eyes and slumped against the window, worried over what was to come. The wind whistled past, as they roared down the street and he drifted to sleep, as he had had an exhausting evening.

"Wake up kid, we're here," shouted Alan, as he reached across the seat, giving him a firm nudge on the shoulder. "You've got all the time in the world to sleep where you are going. Let's rock n' roll," he continued, as he jabbed at Isaac's arm, startling him to wake up sluggishly.

As he gradually sat up, shielding himself from the bright sun piercing through the window; he glanced around while rubbing his eyes disoriented by the terrain. "Where are we?" he asked
between yawns, confused by their location. He peered out of the window, at the thick range of snowcapped mountains, warily searching for the airport he'd flown out of more times than he could count.

John calmly slowed the truck to a stop, glaring back at him without an expression on his face. "We have a quick stop to make first! Come on, let's go, and leave your phone in the car," he instructed sternly, abruptly shutting off the engine and leaving the vehicle.

Isaacs's heart began to race, as he continued to study the surroundings in confusion. Quickly, he jammed his cellphone down the front of his jeans unnoticed, just as his father pulled open his door, coaxing him out from the vehicle.

"Dad, please tell me what's going on…what are we doing here?" he stammered in a panicked tone, while stepping down tensely from the truck onto the uneven ground as he gazed at the deserted forest.

"Come on, you don't trust me? I told you we have a quick stop to make, then you'll be on your way," he said reassuringly, as he closed the door behind him, turning towards a wooded passage leading further up the mountain.

Alan, immediately followed in his direction with a sly look, as Bill stared gravely at him, signaling him to follow suit.

"You guys go on ahead. I'm gonna stay behind and keep watch on the truck," hollered Bill offhandedly, as he leaned up against the truck with his arms crisply folded, watching intently as they trailed up the slope.

Sweat began to bead on Isaac's forehead, as he looked uneasily back over his shoulder at Bill's devious smile, while he glared over at them, until he disappeared from sight.

"Look Dad, whatever I did…whatever I said, I'm sorry…" blabbered Isaac, as he lagged slower and slower behind, scanning the eerie surroundings and pleading for answers. "I just want to go to the airport Dad. Please, I'll go wherever you want me to go, I promise," he continued to cry out, while slowly sliding his hand down his pants and urgently fumbling through his phone for Michelle's number.

John calmly came to a stop, cracking is neck side to side as he fully turned toward Isaac, staring lifelessly at him.

"Shhhhh…now…now. There is no need for tears. Your impact, on your family and this community is going to be one of the greatest of all," he whispered sedately, as the sound of footsteps quickly approaching through the gravel behind them grew louder.

Isaac quickly spun around, shaking with fear when suddenly, a piercing pain went through his spine and his legs gave out from under him. He collapsed, face down in the dirt paralyzed and in agony, as the murmur of conversation around him grew faint. His eyes, closed slowly and his body went cold.

"Please, help me," were his last words.

Chapter IX

After saying good-bye to Isaac, Michelle, was in low spirits as she began the twenty-five-minute drive back home and a constant flow of tears, streamed down her cheeks. As she pulled up in front her beat up house, she immediately pulled down the frayed sun visor, staring at her reflection in the dull mirror. Slowly, she wiped away the streaks of mascara that stained her pale cheeks and breathed in deeply, for composure.

Michelle, finally staggered up the wooden porch, going towards the front door as she glanced across at the rundown property, in disgust. The over grown weeds, consumed the yard and car parts and trash were scattered all around the un-kempt house. Her Father, had bought the house many years before she was born, for her mother, with hopes of fixing it up one day. But after her mother passed away, he lost all the desire and the home deteriorated, just has he did.

The rusted door squealed, as she heaved it open, glumly stepping inside as the smell of old cigarette smoke and stale coffee, smacked her in the face. A few moments later, she heard footsteps and Otis poked his head curiously around the kitchen corner.

"Well, lookee, what we have here! What in the hell are you doing, wandering off in my truck?" he slurred loudly, as he leaned against the wall for support.

Michelle, bowed her head in sorrow, as she timidly made her way to him staring down at the floor meekly. She gently came up to him and planted a soft kiss on his scruffy cheek, but immediately cringed from the smell of day-old whiskey that emanated from him, masked by his putrid body odor.

"Daddy, have you been drinking already?" she asked, as she shook her head in disappointment. She pulled out a stool near the kitchen table and sat down. "It's not even ten o'clock yet," she continued, resentfully.

Otis stared at the floor in shame, before taking another sip form his mug, as his jittery hand shook uncontrollably. "I just had a little bit, to help with the pain in my back. I don't need you reprimanding me," he grunted defensively, wandering out of the kitchen to avoid any further conversation on the matter.

Hastily, he staggered into the dank living room and collapsed on his tattered recliner, fumbling through the empty beer cans scattered on the end table, for the remote. As the TV came on, he gradually eased back into his chair, letting out a wheezy groan as he watched the local news which flickered on and off, due to bad reception.

Michelle let out a sigh of defeat, as she tossed down the keys to the truck and pushed herself up from the table. She quietly tiptoed into the living room and sat down softly on the sofa across from her father, as he stared at the TV.

"I said bye to Isaac, earlier this morning. He left today," she mumbled out dolefully, fidgeting with the sleeve of her shirt, as she hung her head despondently.

The tension eased, as Otis glanced over compassionately at her, as she fought back the tears. Gently, he reached over and set down his mug on the wobbly table beside him. Sitting upright in his seat, he cleared his throat.

"I knew, that's where you were at," he mumbled sympathetically, as his eyes studied her drawn face and the tears running down her rosy cheeks. "It's just a few short months. You kids, will be back at it in no time. Young love, like what your mama and I had, is strong and tough to break," he said encouragingly, with a childish grin.

"I know, Daddy! I'm just still gonna miss him," she said tremulously, dabbing erratically at the corners of her eyes.

"Well, I'll tell ya this. If you guys can make it through this time apart, you can make it through anything," Otis said animatedly, hiccupping in between the sentences.

Michelle giggled softly at his theatrical gestures, followed by an exhausted yawn. "Thank you, for the kind words, I feel better now! I think I'm gonna to go lay down for a bit," she whispered faintly under her breath, as she lazily pushed herself up and began to shuffle slowly out of the living room. "Daddy, please try to sober up. I'll make you a hot supper tonight and run a hot shower," she continued to say, as she brushed past him, making her way down the barren hallway.

She kicked off her shoes, as she teetered over to her bed. She peeled back the throw blanket and drowsily crawled onto her warm sheets, sprawling out exhausted. Seconds after her head hit the pillow, her eyes closed and she drifted peacefully off to sleep and the day crept by. Hours passed, before she wakened to the light from the moon, filtering in through her tattered blinds. She sat up sluggishly, untangling her legs from her bed-sheets and placed her feet down on the cold floor.

Michelle rubbed her eyes, as she staggered slowly across her room over to her cell phone, which she kept on her dresser, plugged into the power outlet. She gazed down at the dimly lit screen, smiling sheepishly as she noticed the unread message notification. She began to toggle through the phone to view the text, just as her father calling out her name, echoed from the bare hallway.

"Are we gonna eat tonight or not?" asked Otis, from the living room, where he had remained perched since morning. His eyes were blood shot, as he guzzled from his cup of whiskey before dozing off again in an inebriated haze.

"Damn it! I forgot supper," she mumbled under her breath, in her panic dropping the phone down abruptly onto the dresser. She hurried down the murky hallway, towards the kitchen.

As she scrambled through the pantry pulling out the cast iron frying pan, she kept out a sharp ear, as Otis coughed and moaned angrily from the other room.

"Damn it girl, where is supper? I'm hungry," he grumbled, as he chugged on the last bit from his cup and threw it violently against the wall.

Quickly, Michelle reached up into the cabinet and pulled out a drinking glass, then dashed over to the pantry and grabbed hold of the half-empty bottle of whiskey that she kept hidden behind the oil and flour.

"Just one sec', Daddy! Dinner is taking longer than expected, but I'm fixing you a drink right now," she chimed consolingly, as she quickly mixed him a stiff drink.

Otis's eyes glazed over, when she approached with the drink. He eagerly reached out, snatching it from her. He let out a satisfied sigh, as he slowly began to sip from the cup while reclining into his chair; then muttered bitterly under his breath, as she retreated hesitantly into the kitchen.

"I'll have supper done, soon," she called out anxiously, as she dug into the refrigerator and strewed the vegetables across the cutting board, as she prepped the oven. Michelle hung her head with regret as she continued to cook dinner, glancing periodically over at the whiskey bottle beside her, before letting out a dreadful sigh. She knew exactly, what kind of night this was going to be.

Chapter X

Mika, let out a tired yawn, as he swiveled his chair away from the fluorescent light, cast off from the computer screen. He began to shut down, after a long day's work at the campaign office. He rubbed his strained eyes as he glanced down at his wristwatch, "9:00 o'clock already…" he muttered tiredly.

After he had set the alarm and locked up the empty building, he jogged briskly across the desolate parking lot to his car, tossing his briefcase onto the passenger seat. Mika let out an unsettling grunt, as he started the engine and began the drive home through the gloomy streets.

"I bust my ass at the office all day for your campaign, you'd think you'd show up yourself," he bitterly murmured, as he veered down the long driveway, leading to their up-scale home.

As he idled alongside his mother's lavish sports car, he glimpsed through the mesh window into the house and could see that nobody was home. Mika sighed, while he made his way up to the porch, fumbling with his keys as he unlocked the front door. He shuffled slowly into the foyer, tossing his things down on the table and made his way into the kitchen, hoping over and over for the remainder of a cooked meal.

"Couldn't even leave me a damn plate of food, either?" he muttered sharply, before pulling the loaf of bread resting on top of the refrigerator down and slamming it angrily onto the granite counter top.

Mika finished eating and then gradually made his way upstairs unhurriedly, as he yawned with exhaustion. He slipped off his work shoes, neatly stacking them onto his shoe rack. He then unbuttoned the collar of his dress shirt and plopped down heavily onto the corner of his bed. He peeled off each layer of clothing, hurling it across the room into his dirty-clothes bin. Then ripping back the thick comforter covering his bed, he crawled slowly onto the cold sheets, wearing only his boxer briefs.

Almost immediately he drifted to sleep, but was abruptly woken up by the loud slam of the front door, followed by heavy footsteps and his mother, sobbing her way into the house. Mika jerked uneasily as he listened to the commotion, trying to focus on the blurry digits on his alarm clock across the room. He stared listlessly up at the ceiling, as the noise grew louder downstairs, echoing throughout the house.

"Mom's drunk, here we go again," he sighed dully, ripping the sheets off him, as he stumbled across the moonlit room over to his dresser. He quickly yanked out a crisp t-shirt, pulling it over his head as he made his way towards the stairwell.

When he reached the living room, he noticed his mother sprawled across the couch, with her head buried in her arms and sobbing uncontrollably. Mika came and sat gently beside her, wrapping his arm around her shoulders, and giving her a comforting squeeze.

"What's going on, Mom…what happened?" he asked curiously, as he stifled a yawn, patting her reassuringly on the back.

Nadia, slowly raised her head up and looked at him with a contorted face, as tears from her blood shot eyes ran down her cheeks, smearing her make-up. Her voice shuddered, as she struggled to speak, while gasping for air. "Something happened to Isaac," she said.

Mika, stared back at her uneasily. "What are you talking about? Something happened to him? Like, what?" he asked sharply, as he looked around the house, searching for his father.

Slowly, her hand rose up and she pointed her trembling finger down the hallway toward John's office, before dropping her head back onto her arms, crying hysterically.

Quickly, he jumped up from the couch and darted across to his Father's office, pushing through the door which was open slightly, staring intently at John, who was standing hunched over his desk. His arm shook, as he held his desk phone firmly to his ear, listening keenly to the voice on the other end of the line.

"What do you mean, he is gone? Where is my son, God damn it?" he cried out frantically, as his voice broke and sweat dripped slowly from his forehead, down the side of his beet-red face. "You're not making sense, just tell me, where my boy is," he pleaded hoarsely into the phone, as Mika stood paralyzed in the doorway, watching intently as he tried to piece together what was really happening.

Suddenly, John's hand went limp, dropping the receiver abruptly to the floor, as his expressionless face turned pale. Mika, felt a knot in the pit of his stomach, as he warily watched his Father's eyes glaze over with tears. Stumbling back lifelessly, he collapsed with a heavy heart into his office chair.

"Who, was that? What, did they say? What happened to Isaac?" shrieked Mika breathlessly, as John ignored him, staring glassy eyed at the wall, with a blank expression on his face. "Damn it, somebody had better tell me, what the fuck is going on?" he demanded, as Nadia slowly crept into the room behind him and grabbed hold of his arm. She gazed nervously at John, dabbing her eyes with a wad of shriveled tissue.

"Is it true John? Is it true?" she asked in a tremulous voice, faltering as her legs began to give away from under her. "Is my baby gone?" she continued almost inaudibly, before buckling to the ground, while Mika held her tightly in his arms, easing her feeble body to the floor.

John, slowly pulled himself up from his chair, teetering around his desk to where Mika was crouched beside his mother. His legs quivered and he struggled to keep them from giving in, as he peered down at them with a heart-rending look.

"That, was the Foundation on the phone. They say that the helicopter Isaac was on, went down shortly after take-off, in Honduras. They haven't found any survivors yet..." John stammered out in dismay, choking the tears that streamed down his face.

Mika's body went numb, as a cold shiver ran down his spine. He felt, like he had been struck with lightening. He sat in a motionless trance, as he listened to his mother wailing out in pain. His father crumbled to the floor to console her, by lying beside her.

Slowly, Mika rose up from the floor, staggering in a daze from the office back into the living room, where he caved to his knees with heartache, his hand clutched over his rapidly beating heart.

"You're lying! He, was just here! It makes no sense," he shouted out confusedly from the living room, as he wept loudly on the floor. "What have you done?" he shrieked out with anger, as he stood up from the floor and paced back and forth irrationally around the room.

Tears surged down his face as he choked, struggling to breathe and he staggered back into the office, standing hesitantly at the doorway. Mika looked down with hostility at his Father, who was lying on the floor consoling Nadia, as she sobbed morosely.

"Are you happy now? Look, what you have done," he spat out bitterly, while cracking his knuckles as his hands shook from anxiety. "All he wanted to do, was to impress you…for once, had you believed in him," he shouted cruelly, as he violently kicked the door beside him. He then stormed across the room to the desk and tore down the framed family portrait that hung on the wall, hurling it to the floor and shattering it to pieces.

John, stared blankly up at Mika in a frozen stupor, as he continued to berate him, knocking pictures down from the wall, all the while crying hysterically. He quickly picked up the phone receiver from the floor, where it had fallen.

"Who, were you talking to?" he growled out hoarsely, while pressing the receiver to his ear, listening for a dial tone. "Who were you fucking talking to?" Mika shouted once more, before viciously throwing the phone against the wall, as pieces of plastic flew across the room.

"Stop it," screamed Nadia, as she flinched fearfully in John's arms, looking up at him for mercy. "Please…stop," she continued softly, trembling in horror, before digging her head back into John's arms, in despair.

At this, Mika snapped out of his enraged state and his heart sank, as he gazed resentfully at the defaced room and then down at his mother, who was slumped lifeless in his father's arms. "I…I'm sorry," he mumbled remorsefully, as he shook his head distraughtly, staggering his way out of the office and down the hall.

As he scrambled up to the stairs, he looked sorrowfully over at Isaac's room, hesitating, before slowly moving towards it. He nervously reached out for the doorknob, twisting it slowly, as he crept into the dark room feeling his way over to the bed. Mika breathed in and out shallowly as he tensely sat down on the bed, looking around at the shadowy shapes of Isaac's belongings, in grief.

Gloomy memories ate into him, as his grief-stricken body gave out from under him. He coiled up limply on the bedspread, blabbering profusely for what seemed to be hours, until exhaustion overtook him and he gradually drifted off to sleep.

Chapter XI

The sound of the doorbell, resonated throughout the house waking Mika up, as he hazily scanned the room trying to piece together where he was. Immediately, his eyes welled with tears, while he lay stiffly on the bed listening intently, as the chatter and whispers coming from downstairs grew louder. The horrible nightmare he assumed he had, was real.

He sluggishly mustered up the strength, to pick his weak body up off the bed. He began to slowly make his way downstairs, to face the reality. His head throbbed, as he shuffled down the narrow staircase into the living room, glancing around at the tearful neighbors and friends, who had gathered to show their support. Mika moved past the crowd and into the kitchen, where his Aunt Diana was slouched over at the kitchen table, wiping away tears as she fumbled through his mother's address book.

As Diana noticed him coming from the corner of her eye, she immediately flashed a comforting smile, hoping to mask her heart-wrenching grimace and the blood shot eyes that dominated her face. She slowly rose from the table and straightened out the wrinkles in her long skirt, as she gingerly spread her arms out for a consoling hug.

"How are you holding up, sweetie?" she whispered sympathetically, while placing her arms around his shoulders and pulling him towards her, as she kissed him on the cheek.

Mika let out a deep breath, as he freed himself gently from her grasp and meandered into the kitchen. "I need some water," he grumbled out hoarsely, clearing his throat as he reached for an empty glass in the cabinet. Diana slowly sat back down, resuming her scrolling through the address book, as he thirstily filled his cup up from the sink.

He, came out from the kitchen and headed towards Diana. Sitting tensely down beside her, he peeked obscurely out into the living room, at the small group gathered over there, to mourn the loss and comfort his parents. He let out a weary sigh, as he ran his hands through his hair looking through the crowd curiously. "Where's Dad?" he nervously muttered under his breath, still remorseful over his outburst the night before.

Diana, quickly picked her head up glancing into the living room, before snapping her fingers in recollection.

"Oh, that's right. Your father left about an hour ago with a few other gentlemen. He said he had to go answer some questions," she replied softly, as she continued to flip through the pages, jotting down phone numbers as she went.

Mika nodded gently, setting his glass down as he dolefully hung his head, nervously fidgeting with his foot before reluctantly looking in her direction.

"And my mom…how is she doing?" he questioned softly, staring warily into her eyes, as he studied her changing expression.

Diana slowly closed the address book, gently resting it on the table in front of her, as she stared grimly back at him filled with concern!

"Not so well. Your father called the doctor a while ago and he gave her some anti-depressants, to calm down her nerves. She is upstairs, resting right now," she replied, as she dabbed her eyes with the tissue she had balled up next to her on the table.

"They say, moments after take-off, the little engine just gave way and they immediately went down. It's just tragic, his life couldn't have been spared," she said morosely, staring blankly down at the table in horror.

"Spared? Were there survivors?" blurted out Mika anxiously, as he sat up eagerly in his chair.

Diana quickly glanced up at him, as she fiddled with her tissue, "I just mean, your mother isn't taking it so well. It's tragic he is gone," she mumbled quietly, ignoring his question.

With that, she slid the address book over towards him, getting his attention. "I've called everyone I can think of. Did Isaac have any close friends, or anyone else you can think of, that you want to reach out to?" she asked uneasily, as she glanced in his direction.

Mika sat back in his seat, while he pondered over the question, before letting out a gut-wrenching gasp as his face went pale.

"Michelle..." he whispered wistfully, as he ran his hands anxiously through his hair while shaking his head despair. He clenched his hand into a fist and he angrily pounded repeatedly against the table, cursing inaudibly under his breath.

"Who is Michelle?" questioned Diana, as she leaned and cupped her hands gently over his fist to comfort him, while she keenly listened to him.

He looked aimlessly around the room, as he struggled to put together an answer. "Isaac's fiancé," he blurted emotionlessly. "Please…please, just let me be the one to tell her," he continued, leaning forward and resting his head on top of her hands, as she gave his fist a comforting squeeze.

Chapter XII

Michelle stretched, as she staggered out from her room and down the hall, to start a pot of coffee. She tiredly picked up the empty beer cans and cigarette butts strewn over the floor, as she made her way to the kitchen. "Disgusting! Why do you do this to yourself," she mumbled dejectedly to herself, as she rolled her eyes and stuffed the beer bottles into the trash can.

She wandered over to cabinet and pulled out the coffee grounds, as her cellphone rang distantly from her bedroom, down the hall. "Isaac," she muttered with excitement, as she cracked a smile while the pulsating ring echoed through the house. She quickly slammed the cabinet door and dashed anxiously to her room, searching through her tangled sheets for her phone.

The ringing stopped as she grabbed hold of it, eagerly scrolling through her call log. It began to ring once again, vibrating in her grasp. Michelle sighed with disappointment, as she saw that the incoming call was from Mika. She took her time answering and she pressed the phone uninterestedly to her ear.

"Hey Mika, what's up..." she said casually, as the sound of wind blowing, came through the receiver.

"Michelle, where are you at? We need to talk. Now," he shouted loudly into the phone, causing her to flinch and she pulled the phone slightly away from her ear, startled by his aggression.

"What on earth are you yelling for? I'm at home, where else would I be? I'm about to make some breakfast. What is going on with you?" she questioned uneasily, in a concerned tone.

Mika paused speechlessly, as he fought back his tears and then began to breathe in and out deeply in an attempt to regain his composure, while she listened intently.

"What's the matter with you?" she asked, on edge, as she tensely sensed his behavior over the phone.

"Just stay there; I'm on my way over," he blurted, heavily breathing in-between words, while his bottom lip quivered in anguish.

"What? Mika, have you been drinking? Daddy is sleeping, and I gotta get breakfast cooked. You're starting to scare me," she responded restlessly, while she continued to listen to him whimpering under his breath as he quietly pleaded to her.

"It's Isaac," he blurted out, as his voice cracked and turned raspy and hoarse. "Something has happened, to Isaac," he continued morosely, while his sweaty palms struggled to grip onto the phone.

Michelle's heart began to beat rapidly and a lump formed in her throat, as she listened on apprehensively.

"What do you mean, what happened to him…? He's okay, isn't he?" questioned Michelle, stumbling over her words as her body shivered with fear. "Answer me, damn it, what happened to Isaac?" she screamed hysterically, as her head throbbed from the tension.

Otis woke up abruptly, hearing the shrieks echoing through the house and he stumbled from his room towards Michelle's room, filled with concern. He came up to doorway putting his head inside the room alarmed, as he rubbed the crust from his tired eyes. He stared, as Michelle sat fidgeting on the edge of her bed, clutching the phone to her ear, with a distraught look plastered over her face.

"What's going on in here, who's that on the phone with ya?" he enquired crisply, as he glared at her expressionless face while she blinked gravely, as if she had just seen a ghost.

"I don't know, something is wrong with Isaac," she replied anxiously with trembling lips, unnerved by all the uncertainty.

Michelle rocked back and forth warily, as she pleaded for Mika to tell her what was going on.

"Please…tell me what is going on! At least just tell me he is okay," she begged desperately, and her doleful voice tapered off as a tear rolled down her cheek. "Please…" she uttered out morosely, in a soft whisper.

After a few seconds of hesitation, Mika pounded his fist against the steering wheel as he let out an agonized yell. Gradually, he mustered up the courage to answer, as he sped down the highway. "I'm…I'm so sorry," he cried out mournfully into the phone stumbling over his words, as he began to feel breathless from all the fury. He gasped for air trying to catch his breath, as he pressed his foot down harder on the gas pedal accelerating the car as fast as it would go.

"Isaac's dead…he's gone," he wailed out frantically, as tears streamed down his face, running down his neck.

Michelle's grip loosened and the phone fell to the floor, as she stared blankly across the room. She struggled to breathe, as her body froze and went numb with shock. Otis looked quizzically, at her listless body shuddering silently on the edge of the bed. He staggered hesitantly into the room, sitting down slowly beside her as he continued to look at her apprehensively.

"Well, what did he say?… What the hell is going on?" he asked her gently, as he jabbed her lightly on the shoulder. Michelle, sat frozen and unresponsive to his repeated nudges. He could hear the faint murmur of Mika's voice coming from the phone on the floor and Otis bent down to pick it up.

Without a word, Michelle jumped up impulsively from the bed, bolted out of her bedroom and down the dim hallway. She frantically ran to the coffee table, snatching the keys to her father's truck and then barged out of the front door, slamming it closed behind her.

The sound of the rumbling engine being revved followed and Otis could hear the squeal of the tires, as she accelerated down gravel pathway, veering out uncontrollably onto main road and disappearing into the distance.

"Who, in the hell is this?" he hollered angrily into the phone, as he wheezed and paused to cough as he was breathless.

"It's Mika, sir, Isaacs's brother…" He tearfully replied, wiping the tears from his eyes with the back of his shirt sleeve. "Isaac, passed away yesterday. Some sort of freak plane accident, we don't know much yet," he mournfully continued, as Otis gasped in disbelief, gradually folding over hunched on the bed.

"God have mercy," he murmured softly to himself, as he shook his head in disbelief. "I'm so…so sorry, son. Isaac, was a good kid. A damn good kid," he sadly went on, now in complete shock.

As the line went silent, he understood what he had just seen and witnessed. He eventually let out a weary sigh, as he hoisted himself slowly up from the bed and went over to the window. He ruffled through tangled blinds, peering out at the dust still settling on the dirt road, as he grunted in despair.

"Oh dear I've gotta…I've gotta go find Michelle. She took off in my truck, and I know she's not thinking right," he said cautiously, as he slowly lowered the phone to his side. Disconnecting the call, he tossed the phone gently on the bed, while he continued to stare helplessly out of the window.

Mika slowly moved his foot from the gas pedal, as the call disconnected and swerved off to the side of the road easing to a complete stop. He hunched tensely over the steering wheel, carelessly tossing his phone onto the passenger seat. He let out a deranged scream, as punched the steering wheel in anger.

He, gradually wiped the tears from his eyes and sat up, running his hands through hair as he glared at his reflection in the rear-view mirror. He took a deep breath, then sharply cranked the steering wheel, turning the car around. Then he shoved his foot back onto the gas pedal, squealing off down the street as he headed back home.

"God, please help us all," he prayed.

Chapter XIII

As Mika returned home, he darted inside quietly through the living room, coldly avoiding conversation with the growing number of people, who stopped by the house to convey their condolences. As he rushed toward the stairs he glanced into the kitchen, slowing down, when he saw Diana preparing coffee for the guests.

She casually looked up in his direction and immediately paused at what she was doing and walked towards him, to greet him.

"How did it go?" she asked, as she approached him looking compassionately into his eyes, while trying to read his body language. Mika, shook his head with a grimace as he moved towards her, feebly kissing her on the cheek and plopping down wearily at the kitchen table, as he let out an overwhelmed sigh.

"I don't know what to do, Aunt Diana," he mumbled loudly, as he slouched in the chair, tiredly running his hands uneasily through his hair.

Diana, quietly placed her hand firmly on his shoulder, while she stood behind him. "We'll get through this. Somehow, we'll come together and get through this," she said faintly, gently giving his shoulder a squeeze, as she pointed to the mourners seated in the living room.

Mika gulped nervously giving her a reassuring nod, then slowly hoisted himself up, making his way out to greet the grieving visitors

Hours went by, as he sat uncomfortably surrounded by old friends and distant family. They reminisced, on stories and fond memories of Isaac. As they made sorrowful small talk, he noticed his mother teetering back and forth as she groggily made her way down to the base of the stairs, gripping tightly onto the handrail.

He quickly excused himself, as he ran over to assist her wrapping one arm firmly around her waist, while he threw her arm over his shoulder. He then, gently guided her to the empty lounge chair in the living room, as the chatter in the room diminished to a soft mutter and the onlookers stared with concern, in their direction.

Nadia peered drowsily up at him, forging a grateful smile, as he delicately escorted her step by step to the recliner.

"I'm so sorry…" she slurred, as they inched along. "I'm just so…so, sorry," she continued to mumble, as tears streamed down her face and dripped off her chin.

"Mom, this isn't your fault. Please don't do this to yourself," Mika quickly responded in a compassionate tone, while he gingerly supported her down onto the cushion.

Nadia shook her head despairingly, as she continued to whimper under her breath, burying her face into her hands.

Mika gazed down at her teary eyed, while she cried inconsolably, just as the sound of a car door slamming outside, caught his attention. He rushed to the front window and peered out through the drapes, swallowing nervously at the sight of his father coming up the walkway.

As John entered the house, he paused hesitantly as he stared sternly at him; then without a word, he brushed past him, going through to the living room. Mika, hung his head with resentment, as he watched him make his way tensely to his office, slamming the door behind him.

Embarrassed, by his father's crude behavior, Mika apologized to the few straggling mourners as he followed behind in his footsteps. Without waiting he twisted the handle, opening the office door and slid in breezily. After closing the door behind him, he boldly faced his father.

John was taken aback by his audacity, but his demeanor slowly softened and he smiled at him, impressed by his courage. "Take a seat, Son," he said calmly, leaning back in his chair and letting out a deep sigh of exhaustion.

Mika nodded soberly, as he inched his way inside and sat down in the chair opposite his desk.

"How are you, holding up?" John asked grimly, as he rocked back and forth in his chair rubbing his temples, as he closed his eyes tiredly.

"I'm hanging in there, I suppose; how are you doing, is the question Dad?" Mika replied solemnly, as he looked over at him with concern.

John gave a dismal nod, while he continued to rock in his chair fighting back a huge yawn. His cynical expression returned as he asked, "Why is your mother not in bed?" and added, "she's on a lot of medications and I don't want her wandering around, talking un-necessarily to people." He glared angrily at Mika, stopping his rocking abruptly.

"Yes sir," agreed Mika, as he stared apprehensively down at the floor. He then said, "Dad, let me take over from here. I can start making some calls, I'll contact the funeral home, and…" He was cut off mid-sentence, with a grunt from his father who shook his head.

"That won't be necessary, everything has been taken care of," John said firmly. He sat up in his chair, looking gravely across the desk at Mika.

Mika scratched his head in disbelief. He was dumbfounded and stared into space, as he struggled to understand what he had just heard. Isaac had barely been gone a full twenty-four hours and the arrangements were already in place.

"How did you? I mean, when did you get the time?" Mika stuttered inaudibly, stumbling over his words as he gathered his thoughts. "How were you able to do it so quickly?" he asked anxiously, baffled over the speed with which things were done.

Just then John leaned over the desk, as he glared fiercely at Mika and said in his defense. "I don't need to explain the ins and outs of burying my God damn son to you," he grated out, as his bottom lip quivered through his unwavering scowl.

Mika stared back glassy eyed, as a lump began to form in his throat. "Yes sir," he whispered quietly, hanging his head, and sinking low into his chair, as the conversation in the room went still.

Seconds later, the desk phone began to ring in its shrill tone, breaking the tension as John gradually eased back into his chair. He frantically signaled to be left alone, while answering the call. Mika quietly got up and left the office, closing the door softly behind him.

As he drifted back into the living room, he glanced around at his surroundings in a daze. His father, was secluded in his office on the phone as usual, while mother had dozed off in a medicated stupor and the huge gathering of mourners had dwindled away, except for a few. The shock over Isaac's unexpected death, was already waning and it seemed that life was going on and no one even cared.

He staggered numbly around the room, observing the carefree atmosphere; observing that the guests who were earlier distraught, made disinterested small chat with each other. Mika perched himself unsteadily on the corner of the couch, running his quivering hands through his hair just as Diana called out to him from the kitchen. She poked her head out around the corner, clutching the cordless house phone. She had muffled the receiver with the palm of her hand.

"Mika! Here, it's for you. I think it's that girl's father," she said anxiously, as she waved the phone in the air, urging him to hurry. He immediately snapped out of his perplexed daze, rushing over to the phone and seizing it eagerly from her grasp. "Hello?" he said warily, as he stood still, attentively listening for a response.

"Uh yea...it's Otis here on the line. Michelle still ain't come home yet, and it's getting dark out. I'm worried about her and I don't have my truck to go find her," he rattled off distraughtly, the inebriated slur, noticeable in his speech.

Mika paced back and forth in the room, deep in thought. He then abruptly stopped in his tracks, as he earnestly spoke into the phone. "I know, where she...I'll bring her home."

Quickly, he disconnected the call and tossing the phone back over to Diana, trudged to the front door.

"Where are you going…?" she called, from across the room. She followed behind him, as he scooped his car keys up off the coffee table. Mika, then yanked open the front door and began to sprint down the walkway, toward the garage.

"Derby Point," he shouted back, over his shoulder.

Chapter XIV

Mika turned on his high beam, as he idled slowly into the grassy ravine of Derby Point and immediately noticed Otis's truck parked in a desolate ditch, a few yards away. He cautiously eased beside the truck and shut off the engine, before stepping out into chilly night.

Peeking inside the empty cab through the dull windows, he made his way to the front of the truck and placed his palm on the hood. The engine was still warm and he saw through the windshield, that the keys were still dangling in the ignition.

"Michelle," he roared, his voice echoing across the valley throughout the empty gorge, as he peered around the dark wooded area. He stood motionless, while the crickets chirped and listened keenly before bellowing out once more, "Michelle!"

"I'm...here..." Michelle said gingerly, from the back of the pickup as Mika poked his head over the edge. She was lying sprawled out, staring lifelessly up at the night sky.

Quickly, he let out a grateful sigh, as he saw her wrapped in one of Isaacs's old sweatshirts, dully smoking a joint that she had clasped between her fingertips.

Mika smiled, as he hoisted himself over the edge of the truck, gently sitting down next to her. He gradually eased back, with his hands folded behind his head.

"Do you think he is looking down on us from heaven, right now?" she mumbled, breaking the silence, as they quietly stared up at the stars.

"Without a doubt," he reassured her, squeezing his eyes tightly closed and fighting back the tears.

Michelle smiled, as she took another drag from the joint and casually passed it over, towards his direction.

Mika, reached out skeptically and grabbed hold of the joint. "I haven't smoked this shit for years, but fuck it..." he murmured nonchalantly, as he pulled a long drag, coughing profusely as he blew out the smoke and propping himself up.

He gently passed the joint back, as he gazed sorrowfully at Michelle's expressionless face, reflected by the moonlight. "Your dad is worried. I was worried... You can't just run away from this, you know. We all are hurting right now, but we need to face this together. Isaac is gone," he said painfully, watching her as a tear dripped from her eye down her cheek.

Michelle, took one last drag from the joint and flicked it over the edge of the truck, onto the grass below and her lips quivered as she blew the smoke into the air.

"I know, but something just isn't right..." she cried out wistfully, stumbling over her words, while the tears trickled one by one down her face. "Something in my heart, doesn't feel right about all of this, I mean how... how could he of...?" she continued tremulously, choking on her words while tensely fiddling with the sleeve of her shirt.

Mika interrupted her as he reached down, grabbing hold of her shaky hand while gazing dejectedly into the distance.

"Isaac, was my baby brother, my only brother," he muttered gravely, as he hung his head, shaking his foot anxiously. "I'll get to the bottom of this, you can trust me on that," he grated with anger, as he kicked against the side of the truck while Michelle nodded with understanding, as she sobbed.

They sat engrossed in thought, quietly in the night. Michelle slowly sat up, leaning gently as she gave him a nudge with her shoulder. "Well, I'd say it has been one hell of a day," she whispered hoarsely, as she yawned with her arms stretched out.

"Hell, is one way to put it…come on, let's get you home," he said sourly, as he picked himself up and leaped down from the back of the truck. Then, he turned and gently helped her down off the truck. Her feeble knees began to buckle under her, as Mika held onto her tightly, supporting her.

"I'm driving you home," he declared while helping her to the passenger's side.

She pulled away drowsily, "I can get myself home," she mumbled aggressively, as she weaved, clinging onto him for balance.

Mika ignored her and jerked open the door of the truck, hoisting her flimsy body into the cab, before moving over to the driver's seat.

He revved the engine, giving it some gas, as he sputtered off out of the grassy trench and onto the main highway. As he turned down the road leading to her house, he noticed the porch light flickering on and off and Otis lying lifeless on the steps.

As they slowly approached, the sound of the engine startled Otis and he woke, jumping to his feet and fanning away the moths hovering around him.

Otis, beamed a toothless smile, as he hobbled stiffly down the beat-up stoop and across the uneven gravel, towards them. Mika cut the engine as he exited the truck, making his way around to the passenger's side, where Michelle slept. He tugged open the door and tenderly pulled out her fragile body, carrying her towards Otis, standing near the steps.

Otis took hold of her, straining under her weight as he carried her to the house, while he hands shook intensely. He wobbled into living room, knocking the trash and beer cans scattered on the couch, onto the floor and he gently laid her languished body down.

When he came back outside, he spotted Mika in the distance, walking down the long dirt road toward the main street, alone! "Son, you sure, you don't want a ride?" he called out hoarsely, at the top of his voice. He squinted through the fog at Mika, who had walked down the path.

"No, I think I am going to get me some air tonight, sir. I got a lot on my mind," he replied loudly, as he tucked his hands into his pant pockets for warmth and continued on his journey.

Otis leaned up against the chipped beam, watching him in admiration, as he headed down the unlit path as the brisk wind blew.

"Thank you, for bringing my baby girl home," he called out once more toward him, as Mika disappeared into the night.

Mika trudged the four miles back to his car and began the drive, leaving him exhausted from the day's events. All he could think of, were the unanswered questions he had, regarding Isaacs's accident and the details of what happened to him. "What, do I do now?" he questioned under his breath as his lips quivered, while he sped down the street. "What do I do now…?"

Chapter XV

Mika, woke up before sunrise the next morning, with hopes to get into the office early and bury his emotions in work. As he made his way down the dim stairs, he noticed a tiny sliver of light shining through the door to his father's office, that hadn't been closed properly. Discreetly, he looked up the stairwell to see if anyone else was awake, then slowly crept down the hall, towards the door to the office.

Nervously, he took in a deep breath as he quietly pushed against the door, prying it open. He then carefully squeezed into the office, plopping down on the chair in front of the desk. He reached down and powered on the computer, as he restlessly tapped his foot, while keeping a wary eye on the door.

As the computer flickered on, he eagerly opened a web page and began to browse through the search history, probing for anything connected to Isaacs's death. Simultaneously, he rifled through his father's personal files and made unsuccessful attempts to hack into his email, letting out a groan as he pounded his fist on the desk with frustration.

Mika slowly leaned back in the chair, thinking of a way to hack the computer, as he ran his jittery hands through his hair in irritation. The sound of water running through the pipes upstairs, resonated through the walls and he knew it was a matter of time, before his mother came downstairs. He frantically scrambled to shut down the computer and pushed back the desk chair, when he noticed a small ball of paper, crumpled up at the bottom of wastebasket that looked out of place.

He hesitated for a moment, as he heard the footsteps from above draw near, before scooping up the paper and shoving it into his pant pocket. He dashed hastily out of the office, shutting the door behind him. Mika continued into the kitchen, where he began a fresh brew of coffee and sat down leisurely at the kitchen table, skimming over a day-old newspaper.

"Well, aren't you up early this morning?" chirped Nadia with surprise, as she tightened her robe; taken aback by his presence, while she came down the stairs and into the kitchen. She walked past him, bending down to kiss him gently on the forehead, as he studied the newspaper uninterrupted. "...And coffee too, what's gotten into you, this morning?" she murmured, as she began to dig inside the refrigerator to remove the ingredients for breakfast.

Mika peered up from the paper with a smile on his face, as he beamed over in her direction, while she continued to sift through the cabinet, for a frying pan. "I've just been so out of it lately, I thought I'd keep myself busy by getting into work early today," he responded, gradually setting down the paper.

Nadia smiled, as she began to cook and the sound of feet shuffling about in the master bedroom, came from above. Mika anxiously checked the time, before abruptly getting up from the table, pushing his chair in and starting toward the front door.

"Mika... No breakfast?" called out Nadia, from the kitchen as he rushed through the living room and began to search for his keys hanging in the foyer, while slipping on is jacket.

"No thanks, Mom, I'll grab something on my way. I want to beat the rush and get in, before traffic gets bad," he replied, lunging for the door, and making his way out onto the dewy steps, leading to the driveway. The sun was peeking slowly over the mountains, as he quickly started the car and drove carelessly out of the driveway, heading toward the city.

As he pulled into the barren parking lot in front of the office, he quickly parked near the entrance and rushed up to the door. He peeped in through windows as he approached, noticing that the lights were already on. He then swung open the door reluctantly, letting himself inside.

He made his way past empty reception desk toward the coat rack, hanging up his jacket as he looked around the office, to see who was there before him. The clacking sound of high heels against the hard-wooden floor rang from around the corner, as he looked anxiously over his shoulder to see who it was.

Brenda, who was John's secretary ever since he had been in office, poked her head out from the hallway curiously, to see who was in the lobby. Her eyes gleamed and she let out a piercing cry as she looked at him, taken aback by surprise. "Mika, what a surprise! I wasn't expecting you in, so soon," she exclaimed, as she waddled laboriously toward him, with her arms spread out for a hug.

She grabbed hold of him firmly, swaying back and forth as she squeezed him tightly. "Oh sweetie! I've been praying for you! This whole ordeal, has been so tragic. Why are you back in the office, so soon?" she asked with concern in her voice, before slowly loosening her grip.

Mika patted her tenderly on the back, as he pulled away smiling down at her, while she dabbed the tears subtly from her eyes and straightened out the wrinkles in her skirt. He gave her a reassuring wink and watched her as she vigorously trotted back down the hall, heading in the opposite direction from his office.

He looked carelessly through a stack of unopened mail stacked on the front desk, until she disappeared down the hall into the supply room and then quietly scampered a few doors down to his father's office, closing the door softly behind him. Mika, quickly crouched down in the office chair and powered on his father's work computer, anxiously checking his watch for the time, as his heart raced excitedly.

As the computer slowly booted up, he began to sift through the stacks of files and folders sprawled out across the desk, looking for anything with reference his brother or the "Movement Foundation".

Beads of sweat began to form above his eyebrows, gradually dripping down the sides of his temples, as he tapped his foot impatiently staring at the screen as it slowly flickered on. Immediately, Mika opened a search engine and began to hunt through all the records, to look for any clue that had a remote connection to Isaac. After multiple attempts failed, he slouched hopelessly in the chair, frustrated over the lack of information as he wiped the sweat from his forehead.

He mulled over on any document that he may have possibly overlooked, before propping up in his chair as he remembered the scrap paper he had found earlier that morning in his father's trash bin. He frantically dug his hand into the pocket of his slacks, delicately tugging out the balled-up piece of paper and unfolded it hurriedly.

His hands quivered, as he held the wrinkled paper tightly in his grip, squinting at the faded black writing scribbled across it. "Dissemblance..." He mumbled under his breath, as he read the piece of paper, trying to recall whether he had ever heard his father mention it before. Curiously, he leaned towards the desk, placing his hands on the keyboard and he began to type D.i.s.s.e.m...b.l.a.n.c.e.

He tapped his finger fervently, as he sat perched on the edge of his chair waiting for the search results, as the computer searched through the files. He nervously glanced through the small window out into the main office, checking to see if anyone was coming, as he chewed on his fingernails spitting the slivers onto the floor.

Seconds, felt like hours, as he restlessly waited for any lead to show up, when unexpectedly a folder appeared on the screen with the matching name. Mika's heart pounded erratically, while he eagerly scanned the room looking for a blank disc, so that he could copy the file. He searched through the column of drawers beside him, until he came across an unused flash drive, covered by loose papers, at the bottom of one of the drawers.

Quickly, he inserted the drive into the port and began to transfer the data, until all the selected files were copied. Mika shut off the computer and frantically grabbed one of the ink pens lying strewn across the desk and scrawled "Dissemblance" across the side of the drive.

"Gotcha…" he mumbled under his breath, as he swiftly pushed in the chair and darted out of the office.

Chapter XVI

Michelle, finished brewing a pot of coffee and wiped down the counters after cooking Otis a hot breakfast. Their house, was close to being foreclosed and she hoped a hot meal would help, in encouraging him to go out and look for some handyman work.

She set the bowl of hot grits and burnt toast smothered in butter and grape jam, onto a serving tray and carefully carried it down the dank hallway, towards her father's room. As she balanced the tray with one hand, she pushed open his door inching her way carefully into the dark and musty room.

She shuffled warily through the room, heading over to the dresser. She pushed aside the empty beer cans and makeshift ashtrays to the floor, clearing a space as she gingerly set the tray down.

Queasy, from the bitter smell of body odor and vomit, she stumbled through the filth over to the window. Frantically, she yanked aside the curtains and jerked open the window, letting in the sunlight and felt a fresh breeze blow through her hair, as she gasped for fresh air.

"Daddy, it's time to get up…" she said morosely, as she turned dejectedly and stared at him lying passed out, entangled in the dirty sheets drenched in recent urine. She let out a gut-wrenching sigh, as she crept closer to him, reaching out with disgust and shaking his lifeless body. "Daddy," she bellowed once again, this time jabbing him firmly with her elbow.

Otis was startled from his sleep. Jolting up from the bed, he clasped his hand over his chest, while rubbing the crust from his eyes in panic. "What...what is it?" he grunted bitterly, followed by an uncontrollable hack as he coughed up mucus spitting it onto the floor beside him.

"I made you some breakfast, Daddy. I was hoping maybe later, when you feel better, you can go out and look for work today...?" she dolefully replied, staring down at the floor as she nervously dug into her back pocket.

Michelle pulled out two aspirins, then pried open her father's fingers dropping them into the palm of his hand. She picked up the glass of water sitting on the tray, passing it over to him. Otis groaned as he sat up sluggishly, dropping the pills into his mouth and sloppily gulping down the water, some of which trickled down his chin.

"Thank ya sugar," he growled hoarsely under his breath, while painfully lowering his weak body back on the bed and closing his eyes. Within seconds, he began to drift back to sleep and the blare of his snoring rang out through the room. Michelle's shoulders dropped sorrowfully, as she turned and made her way back towards the hallway, pulling the bedroom door closed behind her.

As the door gradually clicked shut, tears began to flood her eyes and stream down her cheeks. She leaned listlessly against the door, until her feeble body gave out little by little and she slid down to the ground. She sat there weeping

85

quietly for hours, as she spun her engagement ring slowly around her quivering finger.

"Isaac, please don't be gone. Please don't leave me here..." she pleaded mournfully, as she stared up at the ceiling in despair.

Chapter XVII

The morning of the funeral, was gloomy and the skies were overcast. Mika, achingly slid his arms through the sleeves of his coat jacket and adjusted his necktie, as he stared stiffly at his reflection in the mirror.

The murmur coming from the extended family who had gathered downstairs, grew louder, as more people arrived and waited for the church escort. Mika checked his watch for the time and remembered his missing cufflinks, as he tugged down his sleeve, straightening out the crease.

He swallowed wistfully, as he shuffled through the old boxes stored in his closet, latching onto a red package with gift wrapping paper still taped to the outside. He gently opened the box and dug in, pulling out a pair of silver cufflinks, engraved with his surname. Mika examined them as they lay in the palm of his hand, with a grim smile on his face and slowly began to slip them into his dress shirt.

"You were next in line for this heirloom, brother. You never even got a chance..." he muttered dolefully, as his name being called form downstairs, echoed through the house.

Swiftly, he fastened the cufflinks, glancing once more in the mirror to check his appearance, one last time. Then he quickly trudged down the stairs towards the small congregation, who were standing about in the living room, conversing quietly amongst themselves. As he entered the room, he looked over the array of people dressed in black and making small talk, as they waited for the limousines.

Mika coldly squeezed his way through the mass, avoiding those who tried to comfort him as he sneaked into the foyer, isolating himself from crowd. As he stood at the entrance avoiding conversation, he gazed anxiously out of the small window near the door, aimlessly watching as the cars passed by and waiting for the escorts to arrive.

As John casually passed by, he faltered in his steps at the sight of Mika, standing in a trance and scanning the road outside. He pivoted abruptly towards him, walking heavily across the tile floor, instantly getting Mika's attention.

Hearing the noise from behind, Mika quickly turned around, locking eyes with his father, as he glared back apprehensively. John gave him a rueful smile, as he raised his arms gesturing for a hug, as the family looked on.

Mika resisted coldly, but he was immediately grabbed by the arm and pulled close. John held him roughly, as he patted him on the back.

"I don't know, what your problem is and I don't care. You will NOT embarrass me, today," he said through his gritted teeth, glancing back over his shoulder at the casual spectators, flashing a convincing smile. They, adored the show of affection and then went about their conversations.

Mika, pulled away angrily. He stepped back, readjusting his jacket while he stared bitterly at him. "I wouldn't dare, lose you any votes. I wish, you cared as much about what happened to Isaac, as you do, about all of the attention you are getting over his death," muttered Mika, being sure that this would cause a scene.

John stared back furiously, short of breath; clenching his fists, while his lips quivered with rage. Just then, the doorbell rang followed by an eager knock at the door, breaking the tension between them. Mika slowly backed down from the intense clash that was to happen, as he turned to open the front door and greet the drivers, as they waited outside.

Without any delay, Mika went down the walkway towards the vehicles, ducking into the back of one of the limos and sliding along the seat to the corner, where he rubbed his temples, still seething with anger. The soft chatter coming from the assembly of people making their way towards the cars grew louder, as he let out an agitated sigh. One by one, they filed into the cars babbling casually, while Mika secluded himself from the group. He was riled, by their upbeat behavior.

The fifteen-minute commute to the church was a blur for him, as he stared astonished, through the tinted windows, at the crowds of onlookers lining the sidewalks, to watch the funeral procession as it passed by. Cameras flashed, hoping to catch a glimpse of the mourning politician, as the police escort had attracted reporters from the surrounding counties.

Bystanders waved in the distance, as the limousine drifted to a slow stop in front of the cathedral. The driver gracefully walked around, to the back of the vehicle and cordially began to escort each of the passengers, as they left the vehicle. Mourners strolled wistfully up the sidewalk toward the church entrance, as a low murmur rose in the distance from the spectators.

Mika waited, until the limo was empty, then gradually began to slide his way along the seat toward the door, breathing nervously, before stepping out to face the photographers. Within seconds, he was swarmed by a mass of reporters gathered there to cover his arrival, blinding him with the bright flashes of their cameras and the rapid click of the shutters, echoed out in unison.

He quickly shielded his face, as he walked fast down the sidewalk to the fenced off entrance, where he abruptly jerked open the door and dashed inside, to get away from the press. Once inside, he was immediately ushered into the lobby of the cathedral, along with the others and all of them were marched down the vast aisles to their seats.

The funeral director ushered him to the front row, reserved for immediate family. Mika sadly walked down the aisle, carefully observing the sorrowful expressions as he passed each row.

As Mika squeezed his way between the pews, he gently held on to his mother's trembling arm and escorted her consolingly to their seats. Nadia was dressed in black, covering her face with a veil. She whimpered mournfully sitting next to John, while he coldly stared ahead.

Dreary music blared from the speakers, through the packed room, as the remainder of the attendees shuffled to their seats, occasionally stopping by to pay their respects to the family. As the minister prepared to commence the service, Mika slouched expressionlessly, listening to the tearful sobs of those around him. A gentle nudge on his shoulder caught his attention, as he slowly twisted around glancing curiously behind him.

Michelle, smiled tearfully at him from the pew behind, as she sat restlessly next to her father, who struggled to sit upright and hold his composure. She grinned timidly, dabbing the tears from her eyes and looking at him.

Mika, immediately pulled himself to his feet and turned unhesitatingly, to greet her. He bent down, reaching his arms out solemnly, as she sprang into his arms letting out a sad sigh as they embraced.

"It hurts so bad..." she whispered softly in his ear, as a tear rolled down her tear-streaked cheek. Slowly, she released her grip on him, gingerly adjusting her dress as she settled back down into her seat, with help from her father guiding her fragile body down. Mika nodded sorrowfully in agreement, as he dejectedly turned back, lowering himself into his seat, as he waited for the service begin.

Moments later, the funeral official motioned to the clergy to stop the music, as he walked towards the podium to initiate the eulogy. He slowly approached the front of the room, placing his hand apprehensively on top of the casket, as he gazed down sorrowfully. The room went quiet, while the sea of mourners looked on; watching, as he slowly turned towards the crowd and the music softly came to an end.

As the minister shuffled through his notes, he looked soberly in John's direction. While he paused to collect his thoughts, he swallowed once tensely and immediately delved into the emotional pre-scripted eulogy, followed by readings from The Old Testament.

The lengthy tribute went on for nearly an hour, as Michelle drifted in and out of consciousness, vaguely listening to the tributes as she stared glassy eyed at the casket.

The distant murmur of the sermon echoed in the background, like a bad dream and her woeful trance was interrupted, when the minister called upon Isaac's closest friends and family members, to come to the podium to bid their final farewell.

Michelle was brought to, as Otis nudged her lightly on the arm, startling her out of her hazy stupor and she glanced around the room in confusion. Otis quickly gestured for her to follow along, as Isaac's family steadily made their way up to the front of the church. "Fiancé is family, in my book," he mumbled, as he gave her a curt thrust to get her up to her feet, guiding her with his hand into the aisle. John glared unnervingly at her, as she scurried anxiously behind Mika, following the rest family who were assembling for the sendoff.

Nervously, she poked her head over Mika's shoulder, looking at the hundreds of anxious eyes peering back at her from the overflowing cathedral, waiting the tearful salutations. Her knees began to quiver, as she watched John, roughly grab the microphone from the podium and give a tearful and almost staged speech.

As the microphone was handed down from one person to another, Mika wiped the sweat from his palms on his pants, as he clasped the microphone. He stood lifelessly in the tense piercing gaze of the onlookers, as they waited eagerly to hear what he had to say, in addition to the rest of the family's devoted words. As he stood stiffly, scanning the room speechlessly and unsure of what to say, John inched his way beside him, firmly placing his hand on his shoulder and giving him an encouraging squeeze, as he looked intensely at him.

Mika swallowed as he closed his eyes, breathing shallowly, while the silent crowd gazed in his direction.

"Don't you embarrass me," grunted John faintly under his breath, as he leaned close to his ear, while tightening the grip on his shoulder. Mika flinched slightly, then slowly opened his eyes and cleared his throat, while glaring back resentfully at the room full of people.

"Today we gather, to pay tribute…to my brother. It's with great sadness we say goodbye to a…to a young man with such a bright future ahead of him, who unselfishly chose to use his life for helping others," he said grudgingly, hanging his head low.

Mika cringed with shame, as the weight from his father's hand lifted off from his shoulder, while audience let out a soft and heartwarming applause.

"You did good, son, you did good," he continued to mutter under his breath, before giving him a fake hug as he brazenly snatched the microphone from his grasp.

The audience listened on, as John reluctantly passed the microphone over to Michelle, while she stared feebly up in his direction. As she hesitantly took hold of the microphone, her heart began to beat rapidly and she felt a knot in the pit of her stomach. Paralyzed with anxiety, tears began to form in the corners of her eyes as she cleared her throat, struggling to hold on to her composure. Her lips quivered, as she stood helplessly; before Mika rushed to her side to support her.

Michelle, turned away abruptly from the podium, digging her face into Mika's chest as she wept. He gently took the mic from her hand, passing it back to the minister. There was collective sigh from the gathering, as he slowly guided her back down the aisle towards her seat and groups of mourners whispered sorrowfully, as they witnessed her heart-rending breakdown.

As the congregation watched in despair, the minister cleared his throat loudly into the microphone, hoping to get back their attention. Eyes turned up at him, as he sent the remaining family back to their seats, then boastfully called members from the Movement Foundation up to the front of the church, to close the service as John had requested.

Mika looked at them in shock, as Bill and Alan stood up from their seats and began to move haughtily towards the pulpit, dressed sharply in polished suits. He watched, while they made their way up to the front, clutching arrogantly onto their note pads with devious grins plastered across their faces, as though they were getting ready to address the media.

As Alan rested his notes on top of the podium, he slowly unbuttoned the cuffs of his dress shirt and began to roll up his sleeves, as he brashly surveyed the crowd. A room full of people stared back in anticipation, as he held onto the mic while he cleared his throat; a fake expression of sorrow on his face.

Just as he plunged into the presumptuous closing, he was abruptly interrupted by a frightful gasp let out from Michelle, as she haltingly stood up from her seat. Her finger trembled uncontrollably, as she pointed in his direction with a petrified stare.

Whispers of surprise, began to resonate through the hall, as all eyes focused on Michelle, appalled over her crude outburst. Otis stared wide-eyed, over at her in embarrassment and he quickly tugged forcefully on her arm, trying to pull her back into her seat. He hushed her, so the eulogy could continue while glancing apologetically around the room, as she remained standing, rigid, and stiff.

Michelle shuddered, with her feet planted firmly on the floor, breathing shallowly as though she had seen a ghost. Her hand trembled as she continued to point accusingly in his direction, filled with fury.

"That's my granddaddy's bracelet, where did you get that from?" she stammered confusedly, her voice echoing across the quiet hall, while pointing at Alan's wrist focusing everyone's attention on the piece of jewelry. Otis, loosened his grip on her arm, as he looked at him in dismay. A low murmur, erupted through the cathedral and all eyes focused intently on Alan, and the bracelet in question.

Alan glared dumbfounded around room, speechless over the commotion, as the whispers from people trying to figure out what was going on grew louder, while they discussed with each other pointing suspiciously at the bracelet.

"That bracelet you're wearing...I gave that to Isaac, right before he left. Where did you get it from? How do you have that?" she asked furiously, her voice quivering with anger and charging savagely up the aisle. Otis grabbed at her, but she quickly forced herself free from his weak grasp and continued down the row towards him, with a murderous glare.

Alan looked down, surreptitiously at his wrist and gradually began to lower his arm down, hiding it behind the podium. Frantically, he unraveled his sleeve and yanked it back down concealing the bracelet, then casually shook his head in defense, as he rebutted the charge against him as an absurd accusation.

Uneasy whispers and chatter echoed around the room, as people observed the turbulent commotion play out. John jumped abruptly to his feet in an outrage and whistled for the security personnel, while glaring unnervingly, at Alan.

"This is absolutely ridiculous," John, bellowed angrily, while motioning for the security, his hand waving erratically in the air.

Alan nervously loosened his necktie while he shouted over the buzz from the crowd, indirectly denouncing her claims.

"She is obviously delirious, maybe even drugged. Get this lunatic out of here," roared John harshly, as the guards ran briskly down the aisle towards her.

Michelle ignored him, as she continued to shriek out accusations, while banging her fist on the podium in front of Alan. "Answer me, damn it! How did you get that? It's impossible," she continued to shout in a raspy voice, exhausted form the shouting but still raging with anger.

Within seconds, two security guards grabbed her from behind, powerfully jerking her away from the podium, as they dragged her violently down the aisle toward the exit. Michelle resisted them, screaming out in agony and the crowd stood in horror, watching the chaotic scuffle as the guards were painfully pulling her towards the doors. Otis trailed behind, hysterically demanding that they let her go.

When they reached the doors, they pushed her out of the hall.

Mika watched dumbfounded, as the disturbing scene unfolded and motionless, as if he was in a trance, while Michelle was being hauled from the church; as she screamed out accusations.

Immediately, the funeral director rushed to the front of the church, appealing to the congregation for order, as soft music began to play in the background to calm them down. The baffled chatter slowly began to decrease, as Mika focused on Alan and the concealed bracelet now covered by his sleeve.

He watched, as his father approached the podium, turning his back to the crowd as he curtly whispered to Bill and Alan. Within seconds, the men promptly excused themselves from the platform and silently rushed along the side of the pews, leaving the church in a hurry.

John relaxed, as he took in a deep breath and slowly turned towards the mass of curious stares. His sweaty palms held onto the microphone and he quickly changed the subject, back to Isaac's death. With a low and grief-stricken tone, he thanked everyone for their attendance and invited them to the wake, being held downtown at the event hall, as this was the venue where he held most of his political and public appearances.

Still stunned, over the frenzied events, the attendees rose one by one from their seats and shuffled toward the front of the church. Each person passed by the casket, extending their condolences and all of them slowly began to trickle to the exit, making their way to the parking lot.

The media and camera crew quickly surrounded the departing crowd, capturing their dramatic exit as they soberly filled the sidewalk, still un-nerved by Michelle's outburst.

John called out to Nadia, as he briskly made his way out, to diffuse any adverse statements and to do damage control.

Mika lingered, dolefully slumped in his seat, motionless as the last of the guests left.

As he listened to the uneasy sound of his own shallow breathing, he slowly pulled himself up from his seat. He glanced around the desolate room, making sure he was alone. He walked over to the casket dismally, where knelt gently down on the floor, surrounded by the flower arrangements brought by the sympathizers. He gazed dejectedly up at the ceiling, letting out a cynical chuckle, as his eyes glazed over with tears, reminiscing the events of the past few agonizing weeks. His snicker abruptly stopped, as he squeezed his eyes shut, shaking his head as he clenched his first in anger.

Quickly, he pushed himself up to his feet and placed his hand on the casket and stared down, solemnly.

"I'm going to find out the truth as to what happened to you brother…" he muttered gravely under his breath, "I'm going to find out…"

Chapter XVIII

Mika, gazed wistfully at the casket, as the distant sound of his name being called out from outside rang in his ears, followed by the sound of car engines starting up. Slowly, he turned and ran briskly down the aisle, to the front of the church, where he sprinted past the news crew to the waiting limousine. The driver, stood with the door ajar and he quickly climbed inside, hunkering down in the awkward silence, while they made their way down the highway, to the event hall.

Every few minutes, he glanced over at his father who sat with a cold sober face, looking out at the bystanders still lining the sidewalk, trying to get a glimpse of the funeral procession. His mind raced, as he ruminated on the suspicious behavior he had seen going on over the last week, along with the erratic scene that had broken out at the church, moments earlier. Things weren't adding up, in the details of Isaacs's death.

The limousine, came to a jerking halt in front of the reception hall rattling John from his daze, as he glanced guardedly around the cab. Before the driver had a chance to come around, he quickly heaved open the door and got down from the car and escorted Nadia out. The two, promptly climbed up the stairs toward the entrance, escaping the loitering photographers who indiscreetly snapped photos of them, still talking about the outburst they had witnessed earlier.

Mika unhurriedly lagged behind, following them up the stairs into the reception hall, observing their behavior from a distance. He watched, as John shouted out orders to the staff, briefing them on the seating arrangements, just as groups of somber attendees slowly arrived. The building quickly filled with people from all over the town, along with eager members from the media. Mika made casual small talk, until he was able to withdraw from the crowd, still watching the whereabouts of his father as he spied on him, from the shadows.

As evening drew near and the wake concluded, guests finished off their cocktails, while sharing the last of their stories in remembrance of Isaac. The event hall, slowly began to empty as many bid farewell and went back to the cars parked along the street, in front of the building. Mika, signaled across the reception hall to John, motioning him to head home without him, as he squeezed his way toward them through the departing guests.

John, guided Nadia to the exit as she yawned, tired after the exhausting day, wrapping her mink jacket around her shoulders as they continued toward the exit. Mika quickly got through the swarm of people and approached them, as they walked toward the door.

Nadia glanced back over her shoulder at him, giving him a weary smile. "Get your jacket honey, aren't you coming?" she said softly, as she stepped out into the chilly night.

"I'm going to stay behind and see everyone out. I'll catch a ride home and see you in a bit," he replied firmly, as he guided them down the stairs to the limo parked out front, the driver charmingly waiting for them.

Mika's teeth chattered, as he stood on the sidewalk under the dim street light, watching them as they climbed into the vehicle and pulled off into the darkness, heading back to their house in the suburbs. Without delay, he bolted back up the stairs into the building, where the last of the straggling guests chatted drunkenly amongst themselves and the staff began to slowly clear the tables.

As he scanned the almost empty room, save for the banquet employees and lingering staff, he spotted Alan, mingling with a few of the city's councilors, at the bar across the room. Casually, he strolled towards them, listening to them chuckling as they finished their drinks, while the bartender wiped down the countertops. The pompous banter hushed to a soft hum, once he was seen and the boastful group slowly turned to greet him, as he approached slowly.

Mika extended his arm out, to greet Alan, as he moved casually, while the men surrounding him looked at him conspicuously.

"Hey, Mika, how's it going brother! Beautiful service and great turn out, wouldn't you say?" Alan said eagerly, as he broke away from the group and tactlessly moved toward him. He sipped his cognac, as he smiled patronizingly at him. Mika nodded, while giving him a false smile, as he moved in closer shaking his hand while their eyes locked.

"I've had better days, but yes the service was nice. Huge turnout...Guess how Dad wanted it, so I can't complain," Mika replied sarcastically.

"Hey, I wanted to ask you...what was that scene about, with Isaac's girlfriend, about some bracelet?" he continued inadvertently, while nonchalantly glancing around the banquet hall, waving goodbye to the last of lagging guests.

"Oh that! Don't worry about that! That crazy girl and her drunk father, must have been on something. She's delusional. You know, what they say, mourning can bring out some nutty emotions," joked Alan, as he took another sip of cognac from his glass.

"We made sure, to get her home and safe and we all talked out the misunderstanding. I'm sure, that's the last of that foolishness we will see from her," he continued solemnly, as he stared into the distance, coolly searching the room as they stood stiffly, in the silence.

Mika smirked caustically, in agreement. He noted Alan's uncomfortable demeanor and of his avoiding eye contact, after blurting out his rehearsed answer. They stood uneasily in the silence, until Mika quickly broke the tension by cordially holding out his hand, for another handshake.

"Well, I better get home and check on my mom. Good seeing you again, gentlemen," he said tiredly, as Alan smiled back at him, comfortably accepting his excuse to leave.

As they shook hands firmly, Mika glanced down casually at his wrist and then bidding goodbye to the councilors, slowly parted from the group. Mika roamed casually through banquet hall and towards the exit, as the group continued to watch him, whispering sharply under their breaths.

A knot began to form in the pit of his stomach, as he left the building and quickly began to run down the stairs to the sidewalk.

"The bracelet, is gone," he muttered to himself.

Chapter XIX

The cold air hit him like a semi, as he dug his hands into the pockets of his jacket and began to walk towards the nearest bus. As he turned the street corner, he noticed a few of Isaac's friends from high school, still gathered in the parking lot. Their music was blaring, as they took turns swigging from a cheap bottle of gin, while they talked loudly standing in clouds of cigarette smoke.

As Mika recognized a few familiar faces, he whistled abruptly to get their attention and began to run toward them in the frigid night. Quickly, they shuffled around with the liquor bottle trying to conceal it, as they fanned away the smoke, posing harmlessly as he approached.

"Calm down, I wouldn't care less about the alcohol. Do you think you can give me a lift to my house?" he asked eagerly, short of breath from the brisk sprint.

Abe, who was his neighbor and whose father was a close friend of John's, anxiously agreed, as he emptied out the gin bottle onto the pavement and stumbled unsteadily over to the driver's side of his truck. Mika climbed into the backseat along with the others, as Abe revved the diesel engine, turning up the music and trying to sober himself out. As they peeled off into the desolate street swerving in between lanes, the bass from the music shook the car and the teens howled in drunken laughter.

Mika; sat quietly in the back seat, still distracted over the missing bracelet. He pulled out his cell phone from his back pocket and quickly scrolled to Michelle's number and without hesitation began to text her, 'We, need to talk.' As soon as he sent the message, he received an immediate reply, lighting up the bright screen as his notification alarm rang out.

'Derby Point...30 minutes.'

Anxiously, he struggled with his phone, covering the screen while he placed it face down, discreetly in his lap.

"Gotta a hot date waiting on you...?" joked Abe, as he peered at him through the rearview mirror, watching him while he restlessly concealed the phone.

Mika chuckled uncomfortably, as he shook his head while letting out a sigh of relief, as they continued up the hill, moving towards their neighborhood.

As the truck eased to a complete stop in front of his house, Mika quickly flung open the door, leaping down from the cab of the truck and carelessly slammed it behind him. He pounded on the side of the truck, signaling to Abe and jogged up the dark walkway to the house, as the truck sped off into the night.

He approached the front door and peered in through the windows into the house, searching the living room for his parents, as he entered. The house was dark, except for the dim glow from his parents' bedroom reflecting down the hall and he could hear the soft murmur of their voices coming from upstairs.

Mika tiptoed silently through the foyer breathing shallowly through his mouth, while he blindly felt with his hands against the wall, trying to locate his keys mounted on a hook at the entrance. He ran his fingers over the multiple sets of keys, sifting through each cluster, till he finally came across the familiar shape of his University's emblem and hastily held them tight.

Quickly, he inched his way backward out of the partially open door, softly closing it behind him and darted across the front lawn to the driveway, where he had parked his car.

Once inside the car, he quietly put the car into neutral, releasing the emergency brake and soundlessly rolling out of the driveway. As he drifted slowly away from the house and out of earshot, he quickly started the loud engine, shifted into gear, and accelerated down the street on route to Derby Point.

Mika veered down into the murky field, lit up only by the subtle glow of the moon, as he surveyed the area. He idled slowly through the grounds, searching the area attentively for Otis's old truck or any sign of Michelle. He checked his watch for the time, as he moved watchfully through the grassy terrain, flashing his high beams on and off at the mounds of dirt and shapes, that were strewn around the range.

As his eyes moved over the dunes, combing thoroughly through each stretch of grass, he detected a small red glow in the distance coming toward him. Abruptly, he slammed on the brakes coming to a grinding halt, as he focused on the red glow as it slowly came closer to him. Michelle's shape faintly emerged from behind the grassy hill, as she briskly approached the car with a cigarette clutched in her hand.

Mika gazed out at her through windshield, studying her lifeless expression and the glossy shine of her tear stained cheeks, as she drew nearer, under the dreary night sky. Her hands shook, while she pulled the cigarette up to her lips. Taking in a deep drag, she blew out the smoke through her chattering teeth. Her face, was unsettled as she lunged for the car door, crawling inside in panic, and crouching low, peering nervously out of the window.

"Where did you park the truck?" questioned Mika, as he searched the surrounding area for Otis's truck, in the empty field. Michelle, stooped low in the front seat, anxiously peeking over her shoulder every few seconds. "I…I walked here," she said shakily between short breaths, as she cautiously surveyed the area. "They're watching us, I just know they are," she continued, while staring nervously through the windshield into the murky backwoods.

"Who's watching us?" questioned Mika, as he glanced around the barren field, searching for anything suspicious. "Nobody knows we are here; I promise."

"Mika, they did something to Isaac," she blurted out impulsively, as she sat up and quickly turned toward him gazing into his eyes in panic. "I'm not crazy! The bracelet, that…That man had on…I gave that, to Isaac! It was my granddaddy's and I gave it to him, the morning before he left. He, would never have taken it off. You have to believe me," she cried out hysterically, as her lips trembled in anguish with each spoken word.

Mika let out a deep gasp of air, as he cringed back into his seat, glaring speechlessly down at the steering wheel in shock. He sat quietly for a few seconds, analyzing different scenarios over and over through his head, dumbfounded, while he pondered on the information.

"Are you positive, Michelle? I mean positive, without a doubt in your mind...I need to know," he demanded seriously, as he looked solemnly back in her direction.

"Yes," she pleaded desperately, while she sobbed in the passenger seat, struggling to compose herself as tears streamed from her eyes.

Mika, furiously began to punch the steering with anger, as he stared senselessly out of the window into the dark and empty field. "His trip, never made sense. His death, never made sense. Now, we're talking murder and my Dad's involved," he shuddered in astonishment, as a cold chill shivered up his spine.

The car was quiet, except for the soft whimpering of Michelle, as she sobbed into her sleeve and the low roar of the engine, as it sat idling in the dark. Mika reached down, shutting off the engine as he eased back dazedly in his seat, contemplating on what to do next.

"They, threatened us..." said Michelle timidly, as she pulled her shaky hand to her lips, pulling in one last drag from her burned down cigarette. She quickly rolled down the window, flicking the cigarette butt out onto the dewy grass below, before rolling it back up again.

Mika slowly turned his head toward her, absorbing what she said, as he gradually sat up in his seat attentively, continuing to listen. "When they kicked us out of the church, I noticed a black car following us. Daddy, rushed me into the house when we got home, but he stayed outside to confront them," she said nervously, while tears dripped down from her chin soaking her shirt.

"I couldn't hear much of what was said, but when Daddy finally came inside, he wasn't right. They said something to him…something terrible and it spooked him," she said tensely, staring gravely at him in terror as her hands trembled.

Mika leaned over consolingly, clutching firmly onto her hand, as his teeth gritted with anger, "I need you to remember what they said, who said it, and what did you hear?" he muttered breathlessly, while tightly squeezing her quavering hand. "Tell me, what you heard!"

Frantically, she shook loose from his grip and ran her hands through her hair, pushing back the loose strands out from her eyes, while she reflected on what happened earlier that day. She restlessly began to chew on the tips of her fingernails, while struggling to recollect the muffled conversation that took place outside with Otis.

Flustered, she slowly shook her head blankly and pleaded with desperation, "I…I couldn't make out what was said, I don't know! When daddy came inside, his face was pale white as if he'd seen a ghost. He locked the front door, then closed all the drapes in the house. I've never seen him that scared before," she mumbled, as she stared out into the open field in a baffled manner.

"I asked, what they said and he lashed out at me. Told me to forget about the bracelet…forget about Isaac and threatened me if I ever brought it up again! They said something to him, Mika, something awful, that scared him to death," she rambled out, while she continued to unnervingly chew on her fingernails in dismay, as she breathed in short gasps.

Mika gazed consolingly, as he reached over, gently grabbing hold of her hand and tugging it out from her quivering mouth. He pulled her close to him. She let out a gasp of relief, as he hugged her tenderly and she rested against his chest seeking comfort. Michelle, hugged tightly onto him for solace, while breaking out a blubbering cry. As he rested his chin protectively on top of her head, she cried brokenly in his arms, shuddering from the grief.

"It's going to be okay; I promise. I'm going to find out what's going on and end this," he said reassuringly, as he stared into the night, while patting her on the back in a comforting manner.

Mika held her silently, before gradually moving her off his chest as he reached down for the keys, still inserted in the ignition. As he started the engine, he pumped his foot furiously on the gas pedal, revving the motor.

"Go home, and get some sleep. I'm going to figure out what the fuck is going on..." he mumbled viciously under his breath, as he shifted into gear and sharply peeled out of the ravine and toward the main road.

Chapter XX

Michelle, let out a sigh of exhaustion, as they zoomed down the street, while she used her sleeve to dab the tears from the corners of her eyes. She pulled down the sun visor peeking into the vanity mirror, as she wiped away the smeared mascara that stained her cheeks, while they sped down the bumpy road toward her house.

Softly, she let out a giggle, while grinning slyly she stared down at her phone. "We always wanted to go, to Belize. I'm just happy he got to go, before...well, before he..." mumbled Michelle to herself, before her voice quietly faded, as she smiled rubbing her thumb adoringly over the screen of her phone.

Mika arched his eyebrow out of curiosity, as he glanced over in her direction briefly hesitating and thinking about what she had said. He asked her impertinently, "You mean Honduras...?" as he continued to stare intently out onto the horizon.

Michelle shook her head, as she reached out showing him the text message on her phone from the day Isaac had left for the retreat.

"Isaac texted me, bragging about being in Belize. I think he was just trying to dig his heels in, I guess..." she muttered sarcastically, while she held the phone up for him to see.

Mika, slammed his foot abruptly onto the brakes swerving the car to a screeching halt. As they fishtailed to a complete stop in the middle of the street, Michelle, was jerked forward onto the dashboard until the seat belt eventually locked, pulling her stiffly back into her seat. "What the hell is wrong with you? What'd you do that for?" she shrieked out hysterically, while clasping her hand over her heart petrified, as she looked around in shock trying to figure out why they stopped so violently.

"Isaac was in Honduras, when the helicopter went down. I was there, when my father booked the ticket, I mean…I even helped, pick out his damn seat," he said uneasily, as his heartbeat rapidly in his chest while they sat in the idling car, in the middle of the empty road. Michelle gulped nervously, as she stared tensely over at him with distress in her eyes.

"Mika, what does that mean…? I don't even know what to believe anymore. Was that even Isaac, texting me? Was that even Isaac's body, in the casket?" she stammered fearfully, as her lips trembled with distrust. "Nothing makes sense anymore, nothing is adding up," she continued, as her raspy voice faded away slowly.

Mika, was speechless and engrossed in rage. He stomped back onto the gas pedal, barreling again down the dim street. As he swerved down the dirt path leading to her house, dirt and gravel kicked up into the air and they quickly skidded to a stop. His grim and expressionless face stared back bitterly, in the reflection over the steering wheel in front of him, as he seethed with anger.

"Don't say anything to anyone, you understand? Anyone! We don't know, how deep this goes, or who all are involved," he came out sharply, as he sat upright, adjusting his seatbelt and his hand clenched tightly onto the steering wheel.

Michelle felt a cold chill shoot down her spine, as goose bumps rose all over her body and she timidly nodded in understanding. As she slowly turned toward the door grabbing the handle, she stared nervously out of the passenger window at the house, scanning the area for any signs to show that her father was awake.

As she exited the car, she dug into her front pocket, tugging out her house key and she trampled through the uneven path full of weeds and gravel, leading to the porch. She quickly crept up the steps toward the door, when the tire's screeched from Mika's car behind her, as he sped off back down the dusty passage, towards the street. She peeked over her shoulder, watching the tail lights disappear into the night; then anxiously looked over the dark shadows of the property, wanting to see if she was being watched as she stood frozen under the flickering porch light.

She quietly unlocked the deadbolt and slowly twisted the door handle, nudging it open as she squeezed her way inside the small opening. Without a sound, she shut the door behind her twisting the deadbolt locked with her fidgety fingers, then quickly shut off the porch light.

Michelle exhaled with relief, as she stood in the dark room pressing her forehead firmly up against the cold surface of the front door, gasping for air as her adrenaline rushed. Just as she caught her breath and began to calm down, a loud creak from a loose floorboard behind her, startled her unexpectedly and she jolted around in panic.

Otis, emerged slowly from the murky hall, stomping heavily across the unpolished tiles towards her. She listened, as he tripped through the empty beer cans scattered on the floor, until he reached the living room, turning on the rusty lamp resting on the coffee table. A soft light flickered on and lit the surrounding dimly, as her eyes steadily adjusted to the light and focused across at her father's silhouette.

Michelle's body tensed, as she glared at him clasping her hand over her heart in shock, as she gasped for air. "Geez, you scared me Daddy," she shrieked out, smiling warily up at him as she attempted to slide casually past him.

"Where, in the Hell have you been?" he muttered angrily, in a deep and hoarse tone, as he wiped saliva from the corner of his lips. He moved aggressively toward her and his body shifted to one side, as he blocked her way, gazing bitterly at her. His sunken and blood shot eyes had glazed over, in his drunken state. Michelle, could smell the cheap whiskey on his breath and she quickly turned her head away, to block the repulsive stench.

"I was just…just going for a walk, is all. I wanted to get out and get some air, you know with all that's been going on and all…" she meekly replied, as she cowered timidly, staring down at the floor to avoid any eye contact. Once again, she gradually began to squeeze past him, heading apprehensively down the hall, but stopped, as Otis furiously lunged at her. His shaky arms violently grabbed the collar of her sweatshirt, yanking her back aggressively, to face him, as she struggled to pass. Her knees began to buckle, as she flinched with fear. He held tightly onto her shoulders, propping her feeble body up with his jittery hands. He glared down at her fiercely, wheezing in and out through his mouth, with a manic expression plastered across his face.

"Didn't I tell you to stay away from them…Didn't I tell you to leave this alone?" he shouted out crazily, as he jerked her body close to him and his lips quivered with rage. His rigid hold on her shoulders tightened and his filthy fingernails, dug agonizingly into her skin.

Michelle let out piercing scream, as pain pulsated down her arm from his vicious attack. She shrieked hysterically, in anguish and twisted and turned struggling to jerk herself from his unfaltering hold. "Daddy, stop it! Please…you're hurting me," she begged, while contorting her arm, as she pulled and pushed to free herself with all her strength.

"Let go of me!" she roared, once more at the top of her lungs, as she fiercely kicked him in the groin, causing him to buckle. Otis, cowered in pain, sloppily staggering away from her as she broke free from his grip, bolting down the dank hall to her room. Once inside she quickly slammed the door closed, fumbling for the bolt rabidly, as she twisted and locked it.

She could hear the thud of his footsteps stumbling toward her room from the hall, as she slowly crept away from the door in terror, pressing her back against the wall as she trembled in fear.

She cowered, as the shadow from his bulky shape blocked the light shining from the hall under her door, as she listened to his raspy breath while he pushed himself against the door, jiggling on the handle. "Open up this damn door, God damn it! I'm not…I'm not done with you, yet," barked Otis, in a drunken slur, as he pounded powerfully against the door, rattling its rusty hinges violently.

Michelle, cowered fearfully to the floor, sliding down the wall with her back pressed weakly up against it. As she hit the ground, she sprawled out onto the frigid floor. Warm tears, streamed down her cheeks. Otis, continued to hammer against door, mumbling incoherently under his breath until he weakened from the effort on the door and eventually gave up. Slowly, he staggered back down the murky hallway, towards the kitchen, rummaging through the cabinets and drawers, frantically searching for more alcohol, as Michelle remained lifeless on the floor in her room.

She whimpered quietly under her breath, while she listened to the inebriated sounds from her father, as a puddle of tears formed under her face while she lay on the cold floor.

She flinched, each time the sound of breaking glass echoed through the house, as he cursed loudly, while throwing the empty bottles against the wall in a rage.

The night went on like this, until Otis eventually passed out, while Michelle stretched restlessly out on the bare floor, as her body gave out from exhaustion.

Chapter XXI

Early the next morning across the town, Mika was abruptly awakened by a loud and unexpected knock on his bedroom door. The sound, startled him and he popped his head out from under his sheet, looking drowsily around the room disoriented. He let out a deep sigh, as he wiped the crust from his eyes. Propping himself up on the bed, he cumbersomely fumbled his way out of the sheets, while the obnoxious banging on the door continued.

As Mika cleared his throat and stepped onto the plush carpet, he sluggishly tottered his way to the door, adjusting his boxers as he fought back a yawn.

"Yea…I'm coming," he grumbled out hoarsely, as he staggered to the door, unlocking and opening it carelessly. John stood stiffly in the doorway, staring up and down at him intensely, before checking his wrist for the time with a smirk on his face.

Mika, immediately arched back his shoulders, straightening out his slouch as he stared earnestly up at his father, in anticipation.

"A few of the guys and I, are going to go swing some clubs, down at the Country Club. Get dressed and meet me downstairs in twenty minutes, I want to introduce you to some very important people," muttered John, before turning and gradually making his way back down the hall towards the stairs.

Mika stood dumbfounded, taken aback by the invitation, as he watched his father make his way downstairs.

John, golfed every other Sunday with a few other local politicians, at the city's prominent Country Club and it was a known hangout for Colorado's wealthiest and most powerful people. Mika had hopes, to one day join its elite members, but was surprised by this unexpected proposal.

"Yes sir," he solemnly replied, still baffled, as he watched him descend into the living room and out of sight. Quickly, he staggered back into his room, shuffling over to his bed where he plopped tiredly down on the wrinkled sheets. He stifled a yawn once more, as he hunched over on the edge of his bed, rubbing his temples for relief as he mustered up the energy to get dressed. Slowly, he rose from the bed, weaving over to his dresser and began to rummage carelessly through the neatly folded clothes. As he dug into the drawer searching through the shirts, his hand rubbed up against a hard object wrapped loosely inside a t-shirt, at the bottom of the drawer. Curiously, he held on to the bulk unraveling the shirt and he pulled out the flash drive, copied a few days earlier from his father's office.

His eyes lit up keenly while his arm began to shake, as he gazed down abruptly, remembering the files he had downloaded. He let out a sickening gasp, as he held the drive looking back at all the turmoil that had taken place over the past few days that had clouded his memory. Adrenaline pulsed through his veins, as he rubbed his thumb over the shaky scribbling across the top, as he mumbled under his breath, "Dissemblance…"

Quickly, he crept over to the door surveying the empty hallway, as he sighed with relief before slamming the door closed and locking it. He hurried back to his dresser and began to dig through the drawer, pushing the clothes aside as he placed the flash drive at the bottom. He tediously scattered loose clothing, concealing the drive before pulling out a random t-shirt, then closing drawer.

Mika slipped his arms into the sleeves, jerking the shirt over his head as he paced back and forth engrossed in thought. He glanced over at his laptop, thinking of examining the disc, but could hear his father moving around downstairs, waiting on him to come down.

Mika quickly dressed, rushing from his room to the bathroom where he splashed his face with icy cold water and slicked back his hair, gazing blankly at his reflection. He reached down hesitantly, turning off the faucet and dabbed his face dry, while he continued to glare at himself in the water stained mirror.

"I haven't forgotten you, little brother," he whispered softly under his breath, before tossing the hand towel down on the floor, as he darted out of the bathroom going towards the staircase.

As he trotted down the stairs stepping out into the living room, his eyes fixed upon his father who was relaxing in his recliner, humming contentedly as he read the local paper. Mika guardedly moved forward, as John glanced up from the paper, peering over the edge at him as he entered the room.

Immediately he smiled, as he gazed up at him appraising his clothes, with a pleasant grin on his face. He slowly lowered the newspaper, folding it in half as he gently slid it on the coffee table beside him.

"There's my boy," he said cheerfully, hoisting himself up leisurely from the chair and moving toward him. He put out his arm, firmly placing it on top of Mika's shoulder as he gave him a slight squeeze, pulling him by his side as they strolled toward the front door.

"The guys are waiting for us, let's get a move on," rambled John, as he glanced down at his watch for the time, clutching onto the keys of his SUV. Mika followed closely behind and went over to the passenger side of the truck, where he climbed inside, adjusting the seat for room. Before he could even get his seatbelt on, John started the engine revving it aggressively as he checked his mirrors. Without any delay, he shifted into gear peeling frantically out of the driveway, as he veered sharply onto the road, headed toward the County Club.

Mika, yanked fearfully onto his seatbelt and began to fasten it, anxiously tightening the strap as they sped erratically down the street. The truck weaved carelessly in and out of the lanes filled with traffic, followed by the agitated honking from the other drivers as they breezed past.

"Slow down," barked Mika irritably, as he glared uncomfortably in his direction as they barreled full speed down the highway. John chuckled, as he spitefully stomped harder on the gas pedal, making the car go even faster while he glanced back at him, with a smug expression on his face. Mika feared for his life, as they raced dangerously through the city, swerving uncontrollably into the parking lot of the Country Club.

As John slammed down abruptly on the brakes, the truck jerked to a screeching stop in front of the clubhouse and he casually exited the car. Mika timidly unbuckled his seat belt, slowly making his way out of the truck. He watched his father closely, examining him for his rude behavior. John carelessly tossed the keys over to the valet, as he disdainfully went up the stairs and through the wide archway toward the clubhouse.

Mika trailed warily behind, observing disgustedly this lively and arrogant behavior of his father, coming in less than 24 hours after they had laid Isaac to rest.

Once inside the clubhouse, he lagged slowly behind perplexed, as John cruised through the building, greeted immediately by some of the city's most prominent politicians and affluent residents. He watched in wonder, as onlookers paid their respects to him as he drifted through the clubhouse, including many former politicians with opposing views, against whom his father had run in the previous year's election.

His eyes widened; he was blown away, by the revelation that outside of the public eye and away from the scrutiny of the press, John maintained close relationships with these individuals, who he had taken to be disliked adversaries.

As the attention in the room gradually dwindled, John progressed energetically towards the Choice Members wing of the building, which led out to the secluded driving range, for the Club's elite affiliates. Mika picked up his pace, catching up with his father as they neared the vaulted entryway, which was guarded by armed security people alertly manning the doors.

"Good morning, sir," uttered one of the officers, while he saluted him admirably, pulling down the brim of his hat in recognition, as he buzzed open the doors. John nodded cordially in return, as he reached for the door handle, gently whisking it open and guiding Mika inside. As he swiftly propelled Mika through the doors and into the lobby, he hesitantly turned back and jogged lightly, towards the security post.

Mika slowed his pace, as he suspiciously looked at his father peering back, inconspicuously over his shoulder. He watched his father, hustle over to the guard standing at the entrance and glance discreetly around the room, before cupping his hand over his mouth as he leaned in close toward the guard.

"Nobody else comes in here, do you understand?" he whispered menacingly and glared diligently in their direction, until one of the security guards timidly acknowledged.

Mika, pretended that he was oblivious to this exchange, as John darted back through the doors toward him. Taking precedence, he led him down the hall towards the golfing corridor. As he tagged closely behind, Mika appreciated the brassy amenities on offer in the lounge, as they approached the concierge's desk, leading out toward the range.

Within seconds, they were promptly greeted by the club manager who ushered them out, as the staff loaded their clubs onto the golf cart. They took their seats, in the back of the cart and the chauffeur drove them up the winding plush course and over to the secluded driving range, where his father's colleagues were waiting for their arrival.

As they got closer to the summit, the edge of a hilltop overlooking the wealthy metropolitan city, Mika noticed the empty golf course below them. He peered up the hill, at the faint outline of a small group teeing-off in the distance and as they neared, the group of men promptly stopped as they saw the approaching cart.

"John is that you, you son of a bitch?" blurted out one of the men, followed by a contentious chuckle, as he shielded his eyes from the sun, watching them as they drove to the front of the range.

John smiled as he waved casually in their direction, before reaching over and giving the driver a sturdy tap on the shoulder, gesturing him to stop the cart so that they could step off. As they eased to a complete stop, he jumped impatiently down to the ground, proudly aligning his posh watch as he paraded over towards them with a polished sneer on his face. The group joked among themselves over his gaudy appearance, as he airily approached them, gesturing over his shoulder for Mika to join him.

Soon, John was talking loudly with his associates as they stood in the billowing clouds of smoke, puffing away on their expensive cigars as they clashed their glasses of cognac together in salutations.

Mika sighed, as he hesitantly stepped down from of the golf cart and shuffled around to the back of the cart, groaning under his breath. He took hold of his father's golf clubs, swinging them clumsily over his shoulder as he paused motionlessly and calmly collected his thoughts.

"Son, get your ass up here. I got some important people I want to introduce you to," his father's voice echoed powerfully from the distance, as they eagerly waited for him while conversing with each other.

Mika broke out from his trance at the sound of his father's voice, quickly straightening out his posture. He pushed out his chest, while trudging up the grassy hill toward them.

"There he is," blurted John joyfully over the small talk, as he noticed him approaching from the corner of his eye. He quickly turned towards him while he came forward, holding him firmly on the back of his neck as he slowly pulled him close. The random babble quietly tapered off, as the group puffed on their cigars, prudently examining Mika up and down. Mika, looked back at them diligently, greeting them individually with a cordial handshake as they took turns introducing themselves.

He nervously tensed up, as he recognized the familiar faces of other notable political figures, as they continued to stare inquisitively in his direction, sizing him up with brash expressions across their faces.

John beamed proudly, as he looked at Mika's adept demeanor; watching him, as he stood with dignity while the men drilled him with questions, watchfully sipping their whiskey. The atmosphere eventually relaxed and the group slowly dispersed heading back to the range, where they resumed teeing-off. Mika let out a deep sigh of relief, as he casually retreated to an empty table, breaking away from the loud and rowdy group, as he collected his thoughts.

"Young man, come on over here and try one of these with me," grumbled a deep voice, from across the terrace, followed by immediate hacking as he cleared his hoarse throat.

Mika poked his head up and gazed in the direction of the cough, focusing his eyes on the former state senator, Douglas Johnson, hunched over in a thick cloud of cigar smoke. Douglas stiffly waved his hand, signaling for him to come and he continued to cough deeply bringing up phlegm, as he opened his designer cigar case.

Mika hesitated, as he sucked in a deep breath of air, swallowing anxiously while he mustered up the courage. Douglas, was a former class 3 senator, who owned a few local businesses in the area and was a huge sponsor to his father's campaign. He was one of the state's wealthiest residents and known for his fine tastes in extravagant things, as well as for his greed and shady business deals.

As Mika came close, he was offhandedly tossed the cigar Douglas wiggled out from the case, causing him to stumble in an attempt not to drop it.

"Get a load of these," Douglas bellowed out boastfully, as he ginned from ear to ear, exposing his tobacco stained teeth, while he admired his cigars with delight. "These babies right here, aren't your ordinary American cigars, boy. These here are flown in especially for me, from a business associate of mine, in Cuba. Can't cha' smell the difference?" he said haughtily, as he dug into his back pocket, looking for his torch lighter.

Mika played along, as Douglas peered at him through the corner of his eye, promptly gliding the cigar under his nose and across the top of his lip. He took a deep breath, slowly letting it out while praising its strong aroma with gratification.

"Yes sir, this is nice…Very nice," he replied eloquently, forging a fake smile as he beamed at him in amusement. "What uh, what kind of business do you do over in Cuba? I heard there was some pretty strict regulations to that," he continued to ramble curiously, while inadvertently studying Douglas' behavior as he lit the tip of his cigar, puffing on it repeatedly till it glowed.

Douglas arched his eyebrow, taken aback by his question, as he gradually pulled the cigar up to his lips, puffing retrospectively on it once again. He slowly exhaled a large cloud of smoke, as he smiled contently savoring its flavor, as the smoke gradually escaped from his lips. Seconds later, he let out a cackle and a burst of smoke expelled from his mouth. He caustically chuckled to himself, tensely flickering his lighter. Then he glanced at Mika, in a concerned manner.

"Son, one day if you prove yourself to be worthy, we will be able to let you in on some of the business dealings that we do overseas. At least, that was always the plan that is…" replied Douglas unsettled, as he gazed down at the lighter and continued to flicker it, before vigorously tossing it to him without notice.

Mika lunged impulsively down for the lighter and caught it tightly, seconds before it shattered on the hard pavement. He looked up at him in dismay; taken aback by his blunt action as Douglas stared back at him with a lewd expression.

"If you wouldn't mind excusing me," he grumbled harshly, as he abruptly turned away and began to head toward the rest of the group, as they prepared to tee-off.

Mika, cursed faintly under his breath, upset that he couldn't weasel out any information from Douglas and he hung his head ineptly. He stared down at the lighter and cigar, clutched tightly in his hand. Sighing despondently, he flicked the lighter holding it to the end of the cigar until it started to smoke. He quickly began to puff on the other end repeatedly, until his lungs filled with smoke and the cigar sizzled as it flared up. The nauseating taste filled his mouth making him queasy, as he fought back an uneasy feeling and jogged hastily behind Douglas, to catch up with the group.

He approached the men, who were practicing their swing on the artificial driving range, as they drunkenly clamored on about the upcoming election, flushed from the expensive whiskey which they drank like water.

"Mika, come on over here and grab one of these five irons and let's see what you can do out there," urged John with a slight slur, as he reached inside his golf bag, grabbing the long handle of his pitching wedge and shakily handing it over.

Mika, cracked a faint smile as he slowly put out his cigar in the ashtray, resting on the table, before playfully wandering over towards his father and arrogantly snatching the club from his grasp.

He grabbed one of the empty buckets lying on the ground beside him, filling it with golf balls from the dispenser, before casually making his way over to an empty tee, behind his father. As he boldly dropped the bucket down in contest, he scattered around the balls with his club, making a few practice swings while stretching out his back.

John snickered, as he watched him prepare, before turning and focusing on his own tee, pausing momentarily as he tried to control his balance. After few seconds of concentration, he arched his arms back, gripping tightly onto his golf club. He squinted, as he swiftly swung the club, powerfully striking the ball in front of him and propelling it deep into the grassy range.

Mika watched amused, as he shielded his eyes from the sun's rays, all the while following the ball in the distance until it touched down on the manicured field. "Two hundred and fifty yards. Decent shot, Pops," he exclaimed, impressed by his stroke, before glancing down at his own tee, focusing on his stance as he prepared to swing.

By now, everyone caught wind of the competitive banter going on and quickly gathered around, to watch them begin. They cackled with obnoxious laughter, as they teased them jovially while puffing on their cigars. Mika, hiked up his pants as he slowly walked up to the tee box, positioning himself motionlessly and in deep concentration. He made a few more practice swings, tuning out the rowdy taunts that echoed from behind him.

The deafening noise of jeering grew, made up mostly of drunken and sneering chants, as he made his final approach. After a few seconds of ignoring their distracting ribbing, Mika's sweaty palms gipped tightly on the club, as he jerked his arms back and with all his might and hammered the golf ball, off into the fairway.

The unruly comments that echoed from the top of the platform overlooking the range died down, as everyone quietly followed the ball as it glided smoothly through the air. The men watched anxiously, eager to see where it would drop, as Mika followed it closely with his eyes.

Time stood still, as the ball floated through the air passing the two-hundred-and-fifty-yard post and falling onto the range, where it rolled nearing the three-hundred-yard mark.

Mika let out a boisterous roar breaking through the silence, as he leaped triumphantly into the air, arrogant in victory.

John chuckled coldly, as he tossed down his club in defeat, watching, as Mika celebrated the win. "First time at the clubhouse, and he whoops my ass," he jokingly complained, as he stumbled over to the lounge, to fix him himself another drink.

He ignored the chatter and taunting from his colleagues as he staggered over to the table, grabbing hold of the whiskey bottle and filling his glass to the brim. John leaned over and dug into the cooler, beside the table and slowly pulled out a cold beer, from the ice water. He gradually pushed himself up from the table and shuffled back to Mika, tossing him the beer as a peace offering, with a smirk on his face.

Mika smiled amicably, as he caught the bottle of beer, dropping his golf club lazily to the ground. He twisted off the cap to his beer, swigging thirstily from the bottle.

John weaved from side to side, smiling proudly as he sipped heavily from his glass, staring boastfully over the grassy field as he raised his arm, resting it on top of Mika's shoulder. "This is the life…" he bellowed out heartily, as he gazed out over the lush knolls of the golf course and out towards the twinkling city skyline. "I want you to have this son, that's why I brought you out here with me today. To get a taste, of what I've built for myself. I've worked very hard, for a very long time for this and my plan has always been to one day, pass it onto you," he continued passionately, as he pulled on his drink, gulping from his glass while he gazed off drunkenly into the horizon, with amusement.

Mika listened attentively, as he casually swigged from his beer, slowly drifting away from his father and eventually shaking John's hand from his shoulder, unexpectedly.

"You mean, pass this onto Isaac and me," he mumbled back scornfully under his breath, before guzzling the remainder of the beer disconcertedly from the bottle. John's eyes widened as he overheard his comment, causing him to gag on his drink, taken aback by the brazen remark. He quickly pounded on his chest harshly, clearing his throat as he continued to cough while he stared icily over at him.

"Now you listen to me…Isaac was my son, and he made the decision, the sacrifice to go on his own! You, and that little worthless bitch he was screwing need to let sleeping dogs lie," snarled John violently with a raspy voice, as he leaned closer, infuriated and still gasping for air in-between words.

"I know that's where you were last night, listening to God only knows what kind of lies, from her and that crazy, drunk father of hers. You stay away from them, Mika! Don't go feeding onto rumors and don't go stirring up, bullshit! I won't tell you again, you stay away from that whore," he continued to grate in a threatening tone, as his voice shook with rage. He slowly backed away, still looking gravely in his direction.

He slowly pivoted around and angrily stamped his way over towards the men, who now stood silently, staring at them after overhearing the conversation.

Mika gulped nervously, as he bent down picking up his golf club and dragging it behind him while he drifted inadvertently over to one of the empty tees. He felt their burning stares on his back, as he distanced himself further, moving down the row and avoiding the men, as he heard them murmur bitterly amongst themselves, discussing the clash that they had seen, while he nonchalantly practiced his swing.

As the afternoon progressed and they continued to begin, while finishing off the last of the bottles of liquor; they chain smoked their hundred-dollar cigars, while talking vulgarly with one another into the early evening.

Occasionally, Mika would wander candidly toward the group, digging into the cooler for a bottle of water, as he gauged his father's mood. The tense mood lingered and he kept observing them closely, as they grew increasingly more intoxicated.

As the sun drifted down over the hills, John decided to call it a night and they waited for the drivers to arrive and escort them back to the clubhouse. Mika searched around the area, picking up his father's golf clubs, which were strewn neglected all around. He also collected and threw away the empty liquor bottles, thrown on the ground. Smoldering ashtrays were filled to the brim, with half-smoked cigars and trash littered the manicured turf of the driving range.

He angrily dusted the chunks of lawn off each of the clubs, as he gently placed them back in the golf bag.

Carefully, he slipped each head cover over the clubs, rubbing the embroidered emblem with his thumb, in remembrance. He hung his head low as his eyes welled with tears, recollecting the previous Christmas, when Isaac had bought them, for their father. He quickly composed himself, when he saw the driving attendant's winding up the hill towards their direction and promptly rushed over to greet them, as the inebriated men dawdled unaware of them.

One by one the carts pulled up to the kerb, as Mika assisted in escorting the group down the elevated ridge, as they tottered slowly to the swanky golf carts, reeking of booze. The drivers soon collected their golf clubs, negligently scattered on the tee's and hauled the equipment down to the carts, loading them into the back-storage area.

Mika, lugged his father's clubs down to the loading bay, flinging them into the back of the cart, as he discreetly glanced around to see if he was being watched. Quickly, he hopped into the back and huddled down, hiding amongst the equipment. He gasped with relief, as he had distanced himself from the loud and un-sober group, seated in the carts ahead.

Mika let out an exhausted sigh, as he closed his eyes settling back up against a pile of clubs. He relished the brief moments of isolation, as the attendants continued to pack up the cart, confused by his odd behavior. As the last of the equipment was loaded, the drivers began their slow descent down the dark greens, towards the clubhouse.

Up in the first cart John slouched back in his seat, lazily reclining with his feet propped-up, as they glided freely down the path. A chill breeze, blew through his hair. Gary, the former Sherriff, sat calmly next to him, staring blissfully around at the barren course.

"Are ya sure about this one?" grunted Gary hoarsely with a groggy slur, as he slyly leaned towards his ear. John, peered at him and sat upright in his seat, resting his head back on the headrest. The men sat silently for what seemed like hours, before Gary sat upright, glaring back at him as he shielded his eyes from the sun, eagerly waiting for a reply.

John gulped nervously, as he took a deep breath and slouched forward in his seat, engrossed in deep thought. He let out a shaky gasp of air, as he took one last swig from his glass of whiskey, then with a skeptical pause, nodded his head affirmatively.

Gary grinned maliciously, as he roughly grabbed the glass from John's grip, guzzling down on it before casually passing it back.

"We've been doing business together for a long time John, long time! I'm trusting you on this one," he slurred out hesitantly as he hiccupped, then gently began to rest his head back onto the headrest with his eyes closed. "We all got a lot at stake, so if things so south, we're all expecting you to do the right thing," he continued grimly, till his voice gradually tapered off.

John restlessly listened to him, while he stared at the scenic terrain; hiding his troubled expression, as he anxiously gulped down the last of the whiskey and the cart leisurely approached the clubhouse.

As they drifted to a gradual stop in the loading area, the group clumsily stumbled on their way up the stairs and to the entrance. John pulled himself up uneasily from his seat and began to wobble off from the cart, as he whistled impatiently for staff assistance. He hopped down, onto the pavement and tottered along the sidewalk, till he collapsed in a drunken stupor. He peered around wearily, for support.

As the concierge hauled the equipment down from the cart, Mika climbed off slyly, stretching out his back while he ran painfully over to his father.

"I gotcha, Pop," he shouted loudly, waving his hand in the air to grab John's attention, as he gazed around, disoriented. Mika quickly rushed over, grabbing him tightly by the arm and standing him up on his feet, as he slung his arm around his shoulder. Slowly they teetered, step by step, towards the entrance. Even though Mika supported his feeble body, John's knees occasionally gave out from under him.

"Look Dad, I'm sorry, I've been so out of it lately. With Isaac gone and the funeral and this damn upcoming election, I guess I've just not been myself…" mumbled Mika apologetically, as he hung his head low, while clinging firmly onto his father and pulling him along, as they trudged up the stairs.

"Enough of that," replied John forgivingly, as he said loudly in a groggy tone, "I'm just glad to see ya startin' to come aroun'." I miss Isaac too, but we get through things, we make sacrifices…for the better good," he continued hazily, while patting Mika on the back, as they weaved back and forth through the clubhouse, leading to the main lobby. Mika gulped apprehensively, forcing a proud smile as he nodded in agreement.

"Yes sir, we make sacrifices…" He uttered frightfully, under his breath.

Chapter XXII

Earlier that day, Michelle was startled awake, by the blusterous sound of the screen door being slammed, coming from the living room. She quickly pushed herself up from the cold floor and sluggishly stood to her feet, as she wiped the crust from her eyes. Listening quietly, she nervously tiptoed to her bedroom door and pressed her ear lightly against it. She anxiously checked, for any sounds coming from Otis. As she stood hunched up against her door listening attentively, she rubbed her aching back as it throbbed painfully because of her lying in a cramped position, on the cold floor all night.

Her heart raced, as she built up the courage and reached down to the doorknob with a trembling hand, slowly turning the lock with her sweaty fingertips. She closed her eyes nervously and her breath came in short gasps, as she was afraid of opening the door. She timidly twisted on the handle and tugged open the door, as quietly as possible. She cringed, each time the rusty hinges of the door creaked. She then squeezed through a small opening she had made, stepping out into the gloomy hall.

She held her breath, as she slowly began to tiptoe down the hall towards the living room, focusing on the soft glare of the television as it reflected off the walls. Her legs trembled, as she poked her head apprehensively around the corner, gazing around the deserted room littered with beer cans and trash. Immediately, she let out a deep sigh of relief, putting her hand over her chest. She quickly rushed into the room and over to the TV set and switched it off, silencing the loud blaring static that echoed throughout the room.

Michelle hurried over to the front window and gently pried open the old blinds, as she peeked outside without being noticed, to survey the area. Dust, was still settling in the air, which had been kicked up by her father's truck, when he had peeled down the long stretch of road, minutes ago.

Relieved, she rushed to the front door, locking the bolt before sprinting back down the hall to her room, in search of her cell phone. She quickly scooped it off from the floor and ambled over to her bed, sitting gingerly down on the edge.

"Come on Mika, hurry…" She murmured in panic under her breath, while looking down at the dim screen of her phone. The low battery indicator flashed and she dug beside her mattress for the cord to her charger, quickly plugging it into the socket while zealously awaiting his call.

Her stomach growled, as she waited in anticipation, before quickly springing up from the bed and darting hastily down the hall, towards the kitchen. She anxiously heaved open the refrigerator and began to search vigorously through the shelves of rotten and expired food. As she fumbled, her trembling hands ran over the carton of milk. She yanked it out and began to drink thirstily from the container, while continuing to rummage through the icebox.

Famished, she dug her hand into the bag of lunch-meat she kept stored in the back of the refrigerator, stuffing a handful of it into her mouth, in a frenzy.

Michelle, slowly closed her eyes while she chewed aggressively, letting out a satisfied sigh as she paused every few moments, to catch her breath between gulps of milk. She idly kicked the door of the refrigerator closed and shuffled back through the stark hallway to her room, with her mouth full of food. She quickly went back over to her bed, lunging for her phone, as she anxiously glanced down at the screen, checking for any missed calls.

"Come on...You said, you'd call me first thing in the morning Mika, what's going on?" she mumbled worriedly under her breath, as she slumped down impatiently on her bed. Michelle tapped her foot nervously, as she chewed on the tips of her fingernails in thought; before checking her cell phone once again, restlessly. She scrolled eagerly through her contact list to his number, dialing, as she restlessly shook her foot. Michelle pressed the phone up against her ear, waiting for the call to connect. She yanked it from the charger and paced apprehensively around the room.

The call rang out at the other end, as she occasionally walked over her window, peeking slyly out through the tattered blinds, in anticipation of her father's return.

As the call went to voicemail after multiple attempts, she angrily tossed the phone down to the bed and yelled out in rage! "Fuck!" she belted out sharply, while frantically pacing back and forth across her room in frustration. "I can't do another night of this...I can't stay here..." she said desperately, as she dashed over to her closet, tugging out her old backpack and tossing it furiously across the room, onto her bed. She quickly fumbled through her closet for her sneakers, furtively slipping her feet into them as she laced them up one by one.

Michelle jumped briskly to her feet, rushing over to her backpack and quickly unzipped it. She tossed her phone inside, before darting out into the dreary hallway toward the bathroom, where she candidly began to shuffle through her belongings. She rifled clumsily through the drawers of the medicine cabinet, tensely putting together a handful of toiletries, as she carefully carried them back into her room and stuffed them rashly into her backpack, as her hands trembled with fear.

She jerked open her dresser drawers and ransacked through the dinged clothing, clutching onto random garments, and hauling them over to her bag. She wadded up the clothing and began to stuff the backpack till it was full, as she glanced earnestly over at the time on her alarm clock.

Quickly, she zipped up the backpack, throwing its straps over her shoulder as she made her way toward the door. She looked over the room once more, for anything she had forgotten, then sprinted abruptly down the hall toward the front door.

As she reached the door, turning the knob while she unlocked the deadbolt she was filled with panic, as the loud and familiar sound of Otis's truck came from a distance. Her body clammed up and her breathing became shallow, as she fearfully listened to the roar of the engine getting louder and louder. She gulped nervously as she leaned over to the window near the door, peeking slyly out through the fractured blinds at the jagged path, in front of the house.

Michelle's stomach turned, as she watched her father's truck speed erratically up the dirt road, towards the house. She slowly, removed her hand from the knob and sorrowfully began to back away, from the door. Gently, she slipped the strap of her backpack off her shoulder, as she looked around the living room, searching for a place to stash the backpack. She flinched at the crash of the truck door being slammed, followed by the grinding sound of Otis's boots trampling through the uneven gravel leading to the porch.

Rashly, she shoved the backpack under the dining room table, concealing it under a stack of old newspapers and empty beer cans. She dashed stealthily into the kitchen, yanking opening the icebox and pretending, as if she had just started.

Within seconds, the jingle from her father's keys rattled, followed by the squeaky sound of the door being pulled open violently. Michelle listened attentively, as she fumbled through the refrigerator, concentrating on the sounds coming from the other room, as Otis stomped heavily into the house. He held on tightly to the plastic grocery bags he had brought home from the market and they clattered noisily together, as he plopped down in his recliner.

Michelle slowly pulled the eggs out from the refrigerator, placing them down on the counter top, as she bravely closed her eyes, nervously biting her bottom lip.

She let out a shaky breath, as she opened her eyes and forged a smile to mask her uncertainly. "Hey, Daddy, you home? I thought you headed off, to find work already. I'm starting on breakfast now, so I hope you're hungry?" She called out daintily in a soft and sugary tone, as if the misery from the night before had never happened. She dug into the cabinet for the old iron skillet and placed it quietly on the stove, as she waited eagerly for a response from the other room, to gauge his mood. Otis ignored her, as he sat focused on his chair, tediously sifting through the bags he brought home from the market.

Michelle, continued to meekly listen, hoping that he was too drunk to even remember what happened the night before, as she ardently scrambled him a few eggs and began to throw together an impromptu breakfast. As she finished cooking and quickly fixed him a plate, she anxiously shut off the stove and began to tiptoe out from the kitchen and toward the living room. She peeked tensely around the corner, gripping the plate of scrambled eggs tightly in her sweaty grasp.

She peered stealthily, over at her father and watched him while he sat hunched over in his chair, fiddling through his grocery sack that rested on his lap.

She gulped nervously and was short of breath, as she slowly strolled into the room, balancing the plate in her shaky hand. Her hands trembled, as she clutched the plate anxiously; approaching her father fearfully from behind, in the hope that she would not startle him.

"Here you go Daddy, I made you breakfast," she whispered gingerly, grabbing his attention, as she cleared off the empty beer cans and clutter piled up on the coffee table next to him. Otis grunted crisply, while she leaned down placing the plate delicately on the table beside him. She curiously looked over his shoulder and into the bag on his lap he had been rifling through, since he got home.

She was shocked, as she looked down at his old pistol resting on his lap, next to a grocery sack filled with bullets. "Dear God…what's that for? Daddy, what the hell are you doing with your gun out?" shrieked Michelle, as she warily stepped back distancing herself away from her father. She looked down at him alarmed. "Are you crazy? Have you lost your damn mind? What are you doing with that gun, out here like that? What mess are you about to get yourself into?" she continued angrily, while she kept her distance as he continued to sift through the cartridges, mumbling incoherently under his breath as he counted out the ammunition, loudly.

Otis paused, in what he was doing as he gaped deliriously. His eyes were glazed over and bloodshot, from lack of sleep and the alcohol he had consumed the night before. "You stay out of this! I don't want ya leaving this house today either. Stay in your room and keep all the windows shut, ya hear?" He sternly said in a slurred voice, as he leaned in his chair staring stupidly up at her, until gradually hunching back over, as he proceeded to comb through the sack of rounds one by one.

Michelle's eyes welled with tears and her bottom lip trembled uncontrollably, as she shook her head with distrust. "Daddy," she uttered in a raspy voice, as her voice cracked and tears streamed down her cheeks. "Please, tell me what's going on…please…why, are you acting like this?" she pleaded desperately, while dabbing at the tears streaming down her face, with the sleeve of her shirt.

"Go on now, you heard me! Get out of here," he roared furiously, as his voice trembled with rage while pointing his shaky hand, leading down the dank hallway toward the

141

bedrooms. Michelle cowered in fear, as she slowly made her way down the hall, sobbing heavily in despair at being confined to her room.

As she entered her bedroom, she dolefully closed the door behind her and morosely staggered over to her bed, plopping sluggishly down on top of the tangled sheets. Tears rolled heavily down her face, as she stretched out on her stomach sobbing into her pillow, as it muffled the gut wrenching wails.

"Mika, I need you…"

Chapter XXIII

Mika stood at the front of the Country Club, tapping his foot anxiously, while he glanced down frequently at his watch for the time. He sighed impatiently, as he waited for the valet to retrieve his father's truck, so that he could drive him home and get to Michelle. By now, John hung drunkenly onto his shoulder swaying from side to side, completely inebriated from his excess of alcohol. Every few minutes, his knees would buckle and Mika would struggle to hold him upright, as he chuckled aloud obnoxiously.

Mika was delighted, when he spotted John's SUV veering around the corner and heading slowly down the paved road towards them. As the car came to a stop, Mika began to carry John, to the rear of the truck. The valet attendant quickly rushed to his aid, opening the door for him, as they both hoisted John into the back seat, laying him out softly as he slouched over.

"Thank you, sir," murmured Mika with appreciation, as he reached into his back pocket for his wallet, slipping a $10 bill into the palm of the valet, as he hurried to the driver's side of the vehicle. He hastily yanked opened the car door and jumped inside, immediately adjusting the seat, as he settled in it. He adjusted the rear-view mirror and shifted the truck into gear, peeling off as he tugged on his seatbelt, fastening it with one hand as they accelerated out onto the main road.

Mika glanced back at his father, checking on him in the mirror and observing his unconscious and lifeless body sprawled out in the backseat, snoring intermittently. Discreetly, he took one hand off the steering wheel, as he dug into his back pocket, pulling out his cell phone. The car swayed into the other lane, as he skimmed through his phone. "Damn it," he uttered angrily under his breath, while he clutched tightly onto his phone, scrolling quickly through all the missed calls and texts from Michelle. Once again, he anxiously took his eyes off the road, peeking up at the mirror and checking on his father, who was lying in the back seat behind him.

"Dad, are you up? Hey Pops…are you okay?" he casually shouted out, as he stared back at his father slouched motionlessly, snoring as he breathed heavily. He listened guardedly for a response, as the low grumble from John's wheezing echoed through the truck.

Quickly, he fumbled through his phone, scrolling through the call log until he reached Michelle's name. His finger brazenly hovered over her number, then he dialed it frantically as he gulped uneasily. As he stealthily pressed the phone up to his ear, listening eagerly as it rang, he was jolted by the piercing shriek from the other end of the phone, as the call was answered.

"Mika! Oh, thank God! Where have you…" Michelle cried, through the receiver of the phone overwhelmed with anguish, but he interrupted her abruptly.

"I can't explain right now Michelle. Just get ready…I'll be there in 30," he blurted out to Michelle fervently, then disconnected the call, before casually tossing the phone beside him in the passenger's seat. His heart beat rapidly, as he ran his sweaty fingers through his hair, periodically glancing at his father in the mirror to be certain that he didn't listen in on the conversation.

As they reached home, the SUV jumped over the curb onto the driveway. The unexpected jerk from the truck, rattled John awake and he slowly rose up from his stooped posture. Mika drifted to a complete stop in front of the garage, then quickly shut off the engine as he heaved opened his door, hopping down from his seat. John, slowly opened his eyes, letting out a ghastly sigh under his breath, as he lethargically pulled himself up, holding onto the headrests for balance. He groaned bitterly under his breath, as he slowly rubbed his temples in agony, in an attempt to soothe his headache.

Mika flung open the back door, where John was hunched over disoriented and jokingly smirked, as he gazed at him deplorably. "Come on, old man, let's get you inside. Had a bit too much to drink today, you think?" he said caustically, while chuckling quietly to himself, as he lunged inside the truck clutching firmly onto his arm. John swatted sourly at him, irritably shoving him away as he hoisted himself contemptuously up from the seat. He slowly stepped unsteadily down onto the pavement, harshly slamming the door, while he struggled to balance himself.

"Don't you fucking touch me," he snapped grimly, as he staggered boastfully up the brick pathway towards the front door, and Mika backed away to give him space, startled by his outrage.

"You always were an angry drunk…" he mumbled out frigidly, while gazing over at him, as he stumbled on his way to the house. Mika grabbed his cell phone off the passenger seat, stuffing it into his pocket, as he locked the doors of the truck and hurried quickly up the walkway past his wavering father, to unlock the door.

As he unlocked the door and thrust it open, he turned on the porch light for John, who tottered closely behind him. Mika tossed his father's keys onto the table in the foyer, as he hotfooted it through the living room, scaling up the stairs as fast as he could, to his room. He rapidly moved inside, making his way across the dark room over to his cabinet, where he began to frantically comb through the clothing, until he felt the flash drive he had hidden in there, earlier that morning.

As he crammed the drive into his front pocket, he loosely untucked his shirt, pulling it over his waist to conceal the bulge as he left his bedroom. Mika tiptoed quickly back toward the stairwell, scampering down the steps, then breezed quickly past his father, who had just tottered his way into the house.

John hung sloppily onto the back of the couch, as he inched his way across the living room to the stairs, clutching tightly onto furniture along the way for balance.

Just as Mika clasped hold of his car keys from the key ring in the entryway, he was stopped by the icy rumble of his father's voice echoing through the shadowy room.

"Where the hell are you going...?" sneered the voice, in an eerie tone, as John with his back towards him, continued in his stagger to the stairs, gripping tightly onto the handrail.

Mika cringed, as he froze tensely. His breathing turned shallow, as he slowly turned around, facing the back of his father and he saw his chilling silhouette, from the moonlight shining in through the blinds.

"Nowhere Pops, just going to run and grab me a burger or something, I'm starving! You want something?" he casually replied, as he waited motionless for a reaction, glaring across at him in the awkward stillness.

The silence felt like hours, until John let out a despairing groan, then gradually resumed his slow journey up the stairs. Mika sighed with relief, then hastily turned back toward the front door, jerking it open as he dashed out into the night.

He sprinted down the brick pathway toward his car parked in the driveway, frantically fumbling through his keys as he came near it. Mika flung open the door, barreling into the car then promptly starting the engine, as he revved his foot on the gas pedal. Without delay, he shifted into gear, accelerating recklessly down the drive way and veering dangerously out onto the street and disappearing speedily down the road.

Upstairs, John stood lifeless, as he watched through the tiny crack in his bedroom blinds, Mika get into his car. He gazed out in dismay, snooping covertly through the small opening, looking out towards the front of the house. He stood there feeling hollow inside, as he gazed down at the taillights of Mika's car, as it vanished out of sight. The roar from his engine startled Nadia, as she poked her head out curiously from around corner. She had been brushing her hair, in the bathroom.

"What was that sound honey, is everything okay? How was golfing..." she mumbled softly, while gazing at him curiously as he still stood lifeless, glaring glassy eyed out of their bedroom window. He swayed on his feet, as he tensely grits his teeth in disbelief and his blood began to boil. His legs started to shake with fury, which slowly consumed his body. He shook his head, in revulsion. Taking his hand down from the blinds, he staggered back a few steps, sitting down disillusioned, as his face went pale and his temples throbbed.

John sat speechless at the edge of his bed, unsure of what to do, until finally got up violently and stormed out of the room. In his haste, he clumsily knocked down the decorative pictures that lined the wall, as he rushed recklessly down the dark staircase, with a demented expression on his face. Nadia's uneasy voice, echoed from upstairs and down the narrow stairway, as she called down to him in panic, questioning his erratic behavior.

As he came down the stairs breathing heavily from exhaustion, John hobbled down the hall into his office and then slammed and locked the door behind him.

Quickly, he stumbled over to his desk, reaching his trembling hand out and snatching the phone receiver forcefully from its base. He fumbled with the phone in his sweaty hands, struggling to grip it tightly, as he pressed it firmly up to his ear. John breathed shallowly, as he leaned over the keypad pounding harshly on the buttons with his finger as he dialed frantically. John sat rigidly on the edge of his desk, as sweat began to bead above his eyebrow and stream down the side of his face. He swallowed nervously, waiting for the line to connect, as the ring on the other end came out loudly through the receiver.

Within seconds, an older man's voice answered from the other end, in a chilling tone.

"Is there a problem John?" he muttered emotionlessly, in a grim and unsettling tone.

John's heart pounded as hesitated silently, while his eyes glazed over with tears and he remorsefully bit down on his bottom lip.

"Take..." he said, with a heavy heart, through his chattering teeth, as his voice cracked making him falter. John, squeezed his eyes tightly closed, as a lump formed in his throat and he struggled to breathe. He cleared his throat, pushing himself up to his feet, in effort to regain his composure. "Take them out...All of them..." he mumbled in a cold and sober tone, before smashing the phone receiver down on its base; distraught by the decision he had made and immediately, disconnecting the call.

Tears quickly welled in his eyes, as his knees gave out from under him, causing him to crumble heavily to the floor. He held his hand over his head, cowering in pain as he buried his face in his trembling hands. His body shook as he cried out, squeezing his chest over his heart, while he ripped and twisted at his shirt in delirium. "Why couldn't you just leave it alone? Oh my God, why?" he shouted out at the top of his lungs, sobbing violently. He drooled from his lips, as he curled helplessly on the floor, damning himself over what he had just done.

By now, Nadia had made her way down the stairs and was pounding furiously on the door, demanding him to unlock it, as she pressed her ear up against the heavy door. She strained to listen, as she heard the ache and the whimpering from him, coming through the cracks in the door.

"God damn it, John, you tell me what you just did! What is going on, what did you just do?" she shrieked savagely, as she ponded hysterically on the door with all her strength. "Not both my boys John! That wasn't the deal...not both my boys," she wailed out piercingly, followed by a blood-curdling scream as she frantically rammed into the door with her shoulder, until her frail body gradually weakened. Her flimsy body reeled, as she pressed her back up against the door, holding her stomach in agony as her knees gave way and she slowly slid down the door. She collapsed on the floor in anguish, tears surging from her eyes, uncontrollably. She dug her fingernails madly into the carpet as she screamed, as flashes of fury pulsated through her body, in waves.

"Not my Mika, you promised me...nothing was supposed to happen...to my baby..." she blabbered, as she cried hysterically, gasping for breath. Her faint whimpering was drowned by the grievous moans coming from John, ringing out from the other side of the door.

Chapter XXIV

Miles away, Mika veered erratically down the dirt path leading towards Michelle's house, where he shut off his headlights as he slowly idled past Otis's truck, parked out in front. He drifted quietly toward the back of the house, where the bedrooms were located. He brought the car to a gradual stop, in front of Michelle's window and quickly tugged on the door handle, quietly stepping out onto the dusty ground.

As he looked around the desolate property, he knelt down and scooped up a handful of pebbles and one by one he tossed them at Michelle's window to grab her attention. Within seconds the tattered window blinds fluttered and a pair of eyes peeked through a small opening, out at him.

The eyes, widened with happiness, as Michelle jerked on the cord of the blinds opening them quickly, as she stood there relieved; smiling at him, she signaled that she was on her way.

Mika let loose the gravel clenched in his fist, as he trampled through the overgrown weeds back to his car. He let out a tired sigh, as he closed his eyes slumping over the hood of his car. Exhausted as he was, he began to doze off on the hood due to the warmth and the vibration of the engine, as it idled faintly under him. The night was still and all that could be heard was the low hum of the motor and the distant sound of the crickets, chirping in the unkempt shrubbery that surrounded the property. Within minutes, the brisk sound of footsteps startled him awake, as he alertly peered into the darkness towards the sound. He quickly pushed himself up off the hood and began to search the area as Michelle's shape slowly emerged from the shadows, running toward him.

"Get in, we have to go now," she said, as she brushed past him, pulling him along by his shirt, as she reached for the door handle on the passenger side of the car. Mika went over to the driver's side, plopping down unhesitatingly in his seat, as he swiftly shifted into gear and accelerated off into the night.

He cranked the wheel making a sharp U-turn through the dusty gravel, flattening the loose shrubbery as he moved past Otis's truck and out onto the main path.

"Just drive…I don't care where you go, just get the hell away from here. He's got his gun out and hasn't been right in the head since the funeral," pleaded Michelle, fearfully, as she stared back over her shoulder at the house, making sure her father wasn't following them. Mika swallowed nervously, as he peered anxiously in the rear-view mirror, looking behind them for a trailing car as he zoomed down the road as fast as the car would go.

"My dad, definitely knows something about Isaac that he isn't telling us. He is in onto something…It seems, like the entire fucking city knows something," grunted Mika hoarsely, as he glared sharply through the windshield, maneuvering swiftly though traffic as they sped through the city streets. "I found something," he said, reaching under the front of his shirt and digging out the flash drive, passing it over to her.

Michelle, quickly took the drive, holding it tightly as she examined it thoroughly, struggling to make out the words scribbled on the side. "Diss–em–blance. Dissemblance...I don't understand, what is it? What does that mean?" she asked with confusion, as she looked attentively at him, for answers.

"I don't know, but we are about to find out. I copied those files from my dad's computer at the office. I saw that same thing written on some scratch paper at home too, so it's something important. I don't know what happened to Isaac, but something tells me, the answers are in those files," he replied seriously, as he watchfully continued down the dark streets, looking for a discreet place to stop and look into the contents on the drive...

Michelle listened carefully, as she stared out of the window deep in thought, then impulsively reached over and vigorously patted him on the thigh, to get his attention. She sat up alert in her seat, as she pointed to an approaching street.

"I know where we can go! Make a left up there, at the stop sign. About five miles down, in the next county is a community center, they have public computers that we can use," she said, as Mika stamped on the brakes, making a hard left down the road she had prompted.

As they coasted to the parking lot of the community center, Mika slammed the brakes abruptly, screeching to a halt in front of the building. They made their way inside and Mika skimmed over the guideposts that hung from the ceiling, until he spotted the sign guiding them to the computer lab, on the other side of the building.

"This way," he said sharply, as he grabbed her arm, stringing her along his direction on his way to the public computers.

Mika, lunged for the chair in front of the first unoccupied PC he came across, yanking it out as he settled heavily into the seat. Michelle, searched the area for another chair, before running across the room for an unused stool, left in the corner. She carried it strenuously, over to the computer lab and crouched down anxiously on it, beside Mika. She watched attentively, while he inserted the drive. She tapped her foot eagerly, as she sat slouched on the stool, gazing restlessly at the monitor as the files began to download.

"Come on…come on…" she mumbled impatiently to herself, as her foot shook nervously in anticipation.

Mika occasionally glanced over his shoulder checking out the area, as his jittery hand rested on the mouse, while the file downloaded and a folder icon appeared. His heart began to beat rapidly, as he moved the pointer across the screen over to the file, where he frantically clicked on the encrypted file to open it. All the noise in the background muted to a dull hum, as they sat with their eyes glued to the screen, while pages of information filled the screen. Mika scrolled slowly through each page, speechlessly leafing through the documents glassy eyed, as he tried to understand what he was examining.

"I, I don't get it! What is this?" exclaimed Michelle, as she ran her fingers through her hair, tucking it behind her ears and out of her eyes. She leaned forward puzzled by the information on the screen, as Mika continued to comb through the file tacitly, deciphering each page while he quietly went through the details. "What's this, some sort of ledger or contract? Isaacs name is all over this, but that's not his signature. What's going on, Mika?" she continued to ask, as her distraught voice echoed loudly.

Mika pressed his index finger up to his lips, signaling for her to quiet down, while he peeked curiously over his shoulder, making sure that her outburst hadn't drawn any attention to them.

"It's life insurance policies. Look right here, there is one showing my dad, as the beneficiary. Then over here on this page, it's a duplicate, but with my mom's name on it… My God, Aunt Diana too! Here is another one, for one million dollars alone, paying out to Bill with the 'Movement Foundation'! They even have Isaac, listed as an employee," Mika hoarsely whispered with trembling lips, as he pointed at the pages on the screen in disbelief, while gradually scrolling through them.

Calmly, he sat back in his chair in a daze, as he stared in dismay at the computer. His body throbbed with anger, as sweat began to bead his forehead.

"The entire thing, was a set up. The Foundation, the accident, the funeral. All the tears. All of it, for life insurance money," he murmured furiously under his breath, choking back on tears as he continued to subtly browse through the pages on the monitor, as though in a trance.

Tears immediately began to stream from Michelle's eyes as she leaned, throwing her arms around his neck and squeezing him tightly, as she buried her head into his shoulder, sobbing in agony.

Mika remained engrossed, rereading the information in front of him stoically, as she continued to cry against him until the side of his shirt was drenched with her tears. His heartbeat raced and adrenaline pulsated through his veins, as he sat dazed in his seat, paralyzed by what he had discovered.

Coldly, he pushed her off him, as he rose up from his chair hastily, reaching for the flash drive and yanking it from the port as his hands shook with fury.

Michelle swayed weakly, as she cowered over on the stool, dabbing at the flow of tears streaming from her eyes. She slowly looked up at him as her voice began to break, while he towered over her with a crazed expression.

"Where are we going to go? What are we going to do now?" she whimpered in shaky voice, hanging her head low as she was totally devastated.

Mika lunged down violently and held her firmly by the arm, as he yanked her up from the stool, balancing her feeble body while she rocked from side to side overcome with grief. He gripped powerfully onto her shoulders holding her up, as he stared sharply down at her, while she woefully looked up at him.

"You, tell me! What was the next plan? Kill me off too? He said bitterly, while he gritted his teeth with intensity and stared down at her fiercely, as if he was deranged.

Michelle, peered blankly back up at him, speechless from his accusation as he continued to stare at her, with rage in his eyes. He tightened his grip on her arms while pulling her close, shaking her body fiercely as he leaned toward her ear. "Are you in on this too, huh? Are you? Do you get a cut of the money too Michelle?" he growled savagely. His arms shook, as he crushed her painfully in his grasp.

"What? No…How could you think that? Stop it…Mika, you're hurting me! Let me go," pleaded Michelle, as her voice shuddered in pain. She squirmed and pulled, struggling to free herself from his crushing grip. By now, the room had gone quiet as a dozen set of eyes stared with concern in their direction, while sharply whispering amongst themselves.

Mika gently released his hold on her arms, as she jerked away from him, running back towards the entrance, crying sorrowfully.

He watched meekly, as she ran towards the door in tears, hanging his head ruefully, in shame. He pushed in his chair and began to follow her toward the exit, ignoring the harsh comments thrown at him by the uneasy onlookers, as he hurried behind her. As he emerged from the building and ran down the poorly lit sidewalk, he made his way towards the parking lot, searching for her. He looked around concerned in the dim stretch surrounding his car, dolefully shouting out her name, as remorse and guilt consumed him.

"Michelle! Please! I'm sorry," he shouted regretfully, while he slowly wandered around the parked cars, searching through the dingy lot, flickering with fluorescent street lights. "Come on! You know I didn't mean it! I'm sorry," he continued to shout out sadly, as he stumbled hopelessly over to his car, where he collapsed weakly on the cold pavement.

He then stood, stooped dejectedly against the side of his car, banging the back of his head despairingly against the door, as he mumbled under his breath, pleading softly to himself while he ran his sweaty fingers through his hair. "Michelle, please don't leave me…God please…Help me…" he begged pitifully, as he tilted his head back staring up at the stars, as they glowed dimly above him in the night sky.

"Please, don't leave me alone through this…"

Chapter XXV

Hours passed, as Mika stared fixedly up at the dark sky with thoughts of suicide racing through his head, as he sprawled out on the ground in the stillness of the night. The sound of passing cars echoed in the distance and Michelle was nowhere to be found. Mika let out a deep sigh, as he breathed out in anguish. He slowly leaned forward, picking his limp body up from the cold pavement. He fumbled numbly through his pockets for his keys, as he wallowed in self-pity. He then moved slowly around to the driver's side of the car.

As he sifted through the keys, he heard footsteps trampling through dead leaves and gravel, coming from around the corner of the community center. He looked cautiously in the direction of the noise, surveying the area alertly as he tried to make out who was coming. He continued to aimlessly sift through his keys to unlock the car door, when a voice shouted out from the shadows.

"Mika, wait," echoed across the parking lot, as a soft shape emerged from the shadows around the building, gradually moving toward him. "Wait for me…please," she shouted haltingly, scampering through the patches of dead grass that led to the parking lot, as she quickly ran toward the car. "We have to stay together. We can't...I mean...I can't go through this without you," she mumbled, dabbing at the tears in her eyes as she drew near hesitantly.

Mika sprang eagerly towards her, grabbing her gently by her loose clothes and pulling her towards his chest. He gently pressed against her warm body, holding her passionately in his arms, while he sobbed out humbly. "I don't know what came over me. I'm...I'm so sorry. I...I...I'm losing my fucking mind with all of this Michelle," he stuttered out in panic into her ear, as he held her close, gaping up at the sky, disoriented and full of emotion.

Michelle pushed forcefully against him prying loose from his hold, as she looked zealously up at him. "Mika, look at me..." she said solemnly, as she gently reached up, delicately stroking the back of her hand down the side of his cheek to get his attention.

He slowly lowered his head, from his fixed stare up at the night sky, looking down earnestly at her as they stood under the flickering lights. She smiled back at him daintily, while she softly brushed his untamed curls out from his eyes as a breeze blew through the air.

"Mika, all we have is each other right now. We have to stay together through this. You have to be strong for me...please..." she whispered sincerely, as she continued to stroke the back of her hand lightly down the side of his jaw line, while staring fixedly into his eyes.

They stood timidly under the flickering streetlights that dimly lit up the area, as they stared guardedly into each other's eyes. Mika began to gently caress her lips with his fingertips, as he looked intimately at her, while he admired her beauty and at that moment adoring her. Her heart began to beat uncontrollably as she gently closed her eyes, feeling the warmth of his body get closer as he pressed tenderly against her. He ran his hand delicately through her hair, looking lustfully down at her, before slowly tilting her head back as he passionately kissed her on her lips.

Michelle wrapped her arms hesitantly around his shoulders, as they kissed intimately under the fluorescent lights. As they blindly caressed one another, Mika's hand gradually slid up the small of her back under her blouse, reaching for the clasp of her bra strap, where he began to fumble around with the hook. Immediately, she moved squeamishly and slowly pulled away, gently pushing him off while she timidly hung her head low with shame, as she stared at the ground.

"I can't do this, I'm sorry! Please just please just take me back home," she mumbled out shyly, filled with remorse as she staggered confusedly over to the passenger side of the car.

Mika let out a sigh of regret, as he staggered slowly behind her, unlocking the door as she anxiously crawled inside, looking shamefully out of the front window. He frowned as he closed the door, then reluctantly made his way around the car, nervously climbing into the driver's seat. As he began to put on his seatbelt he paused, glancing gingerly toward her in the hope of making eye contact. He gulped apprehensively, as he saw her sitting frozen, looking dismally in the opposite direction.

"Michelle, look," he stuttered, as he sank sheepishly into his seat. He fidgeted restlessly with his key chain, searching for the right words to say to break the uncomfortable silence.

"Please Just don't…I don't want to talk about it. Please just drive," she interrupted, as she slouched, ashamed at what had happened and staring demoralized into the distance.

Mika ruefully nodded, while he inserted the key into the ignition turning it slowly, until engine roared. He hunched tensely over the steering wheel, staring blankly out of the windshield as he revved the engine, pumping the gas pedal with his foot, giving the car some gas. Gloomily he shifted into gear and veered swiftly through the parking lot, turning back onto the main road as he headed back towards the town.

Chapter XXVI

Mika gazed woodenly through the window, as they drove down the dark and empty streets towards her house. As they idled closer to the run-down house, he noticed the flickering lights from the television in the living room, shining through the cracks in the tattered blinds. He slowly eased to a stop in front of the porch, where he sluggishly shifted the gear into parking mode. He glanced sheepishly at Michelle, as she unfastened her seatbelt and began to exit the car.

"I...I need to..." he murmured reluctantly, before stopping to clear his throat as his voice broke in his nervousness and he slumped back in his seat. He let out a deep sigh, as he stared down confusedly at the dashboard, as he struggled to collect his thoughts. He felt the Michelle's piercing gaze, as she paused staring attentively at him.

"I'm going back home to confront my dad. Get the truth out... I want to hear, from his own mouth...His words," he continued to say, before angrily pounding his fist against the steering wheel with resentment.

Michelle froze motionless, pondering over his words, before loosening her firm grip on the door handle and slowly relaxing back into her seat.

"What do I do?" she whispered shakily, as she peered out of the window, fearfully searching her house for signs of her father. Mika gradually turned towards her, watching her while she stared at the house anxiously, terrified of what was waiting for her inside.

"You have stay here. You'll be safer here, than with me. Tell Otis, of what's going on and you both get some things together. I'll be back to get you, soon and we will get the hell away from here, until the police are involved," he said icily, as his eyes studied her hollow expression.

Michelle gulped nervously, followed by an unconvinced nod, while her jittery hand reached for the door handle once again to nudge it open.

She stepped cautiously out onto the patchy gravel in front of the house, gently closing the door behind her while a cold breeze blew through her hair. She tiptoed warily up the creaky porch stairs leading to the doorway, hesitantly, as she glanced suspiciously over her shoulder every few seconds. Mika remained in the car as it idled, watching her as he scoured the area, to make sure they weren't being followed.

Michelle let out a shaky breath, as she stood in front of the door. She stared anxiously down at the handle, then tightly closed her eyes while extending her trembling hand. As she gently twisted the doorknob and quietly let herself in, she was overwhelmed by the sound of blaring static coming from the TV in the living room. The sound, was piercingly loud and she cringed in pain. She quickly cowered down and cupped her hands over her ears to block the loud noise, as her eyes scanned the room looking for of her father.

"Daddy!…Daddy?" she shouted out over the noise, as she eased her way inside the living room, rummaging through the empty beer cans and trash for the remote to turn off the TV. After seconds of searching, while she continued to block her ears from the deafening noise, she quickly put her hand behind the TV stand and began to fumble urgently through the wires and tangled cords. Anxiously, she felt around for the power cord of the TV and grabbed hold of the cord and yanked it from the outlet, shutting off the loud noise that was echoing through the house.

She gradually pulled herself up, from behind the TV set and inched her way back though the trashed living room. She looked suspiciously down the stretch of the pitch-black hallway, leading to the bedrooms.

"Daddy…listen, I'm sorry I snuck out, but I need to speak to you and it's very important. Please don't be angry…" she called out submissively, while she continued to walk through the living room apprehensively. She screened the kitchen as she passed by, heading down the murky hallway, towards the bedroom.

Empty bottles were strewed across the floor, as she struggled to maneuver through them, flipping on the light switch once she reached the wall. The lucent light bulb flickered on and off before burning out, as she proceeded down the dark hall towards the rooms. As she reached Otis's room she pressed her hand delicately up against the door, nudging it slightly open as she peered shyly inside the grim and dusky room.

"Daddy, you asleep?" she called out in an unsettled tone, as she struggled to squeeze through the small opening, forcing the door open and shoving aside the clutter of dirty clothes and scattered belongings.

Michelle paused cautiously in the doorway, as she glided her trembling hand along the inside wall, frantically feeling around for the light switch. She continued to mutter uneasily, as her eyes skimmed across the odd shapes lying in disarray around the room.

"Why aren't you answering me? What is going on with you today?" she called out, sternly, as she fumbled with her fingertips along the wall for the switch, trying to figure out what had happened in the ransacked room.

As she anxiously felt her hand over the switch and flipped it on, she warily scanned through the ravaged room, while the light slowly glimmered on to a dull glow. As her eyes gradually adjusted to the light, she immediately zeroed in on her father's limp body slumped over on the bed, in the center of the room. She froze, as she gazed at him lying face down in a thick pool of blood, with his pistol held loosely in his pale hand, surrounded by an array of bullets strewn chaotically on the floor below.

The room, had been pillaged and the acrid odor of coagulated blood and burnt flesh, floated subtly in the air.

"Oh my God... Daddy!" Michelle screamed, as she desperately ploughed her way through the debris of clothing and detached drawers and struggled to make her way over to his body. She quickly lunged for the bed, grabbing him furiously by the shoulder, as she began to turn his lethargic body on to his back. She tugged with all her strength, to get him to turn. She immediately reached her shaky hand up to his blood-soaked neck, pressing down firmly under his jaw as she felt hysterically for a pulse on his cold body.

"Daddy...Please...No..." she whimpered morosely, after a few seconds of probing his body for a heartbeat. She gradually released her grip on his flimsy wrist, hopelessly stumbling away from his stiff body, as she slowly shook her head in shock. Deliriously, she staggered backwards, bracing herself on the corner of his bedframe. The room spun, as she gazed down at the gaping hole that mutilated the side of his face, making it unrecognizable. She squirmed erratically, at the sight of her father's disfigured body, while wheezing hoarsely as she inched her way further away from the room.

Frantically, she let out a blood-curdling scream, which echoed down the grisly hallway and throughout the entire house. She quickly turned and stumbled back toward the doorway in a frenzy; tripping over the wreckage on the floor as she fell to her knees. She panted uncontrollably, as she crawled hysterically out of the bedroom and back into the hall.

As she dragged her quavering self from the room, she faltered along the way as she vomited, gasping for air and struggling to breathe.

As Michelle continued to scream distraughtly in between breaths, her weak body gave out from under her causing her to collapse in shock, toppling face down and unconscious on the floor.

"Help...me..." were her last words, before passing out.

Chapter XXVII

Mika sat hunched dejectedly over the steering wheel, contemplating on how he would confront his father, as the car's engine softly hummed beneath him. Elements of doubt swarmed his mind, as he struggled to muster up the courage to face the nightmare head on. Just as he prepared to take off, he was startled abruptly by the muffled sounds of screaming, coming from inside the house.

"Michelle…" he whispered under his breath with concern, as he furiously unfastened his seat belt, barreling carelessly out of car. He frantically raced up the dusty path towards the house, climbing as fast as he could, up the porch steps to the door. Without hesitation he jumped up powerfully, kicking the door open and breaking it loose from its hinges, as he ran anxiously into the house.

Once inside he immediately zeroed on Michelle's flimsy body, lying motionless in the shadows on the bare, decaying floor. He rushed quickly over to her, kneeling down beside her, as he grabbed hold of her helpless frame and gently cradling his hands under her neck for support.

"What happened baby…Come on now, wake up…Michelle?" he called out uneasily, as he stared down intently at her frail body. He pulled her torso up from off the dirty floor and began to rock her softly in his arms, while firmly shaking her.

Gradually, her eyes began to flutter open and she moaned sluggishly, while Mika continued to call out to her as she drowsily regained consciousness. She mumbled incoherently back to him, struggling to form a complete sentence, as he held her tired body vigilantly in his arms.

"What the hell happened to you?" exclaimed Mika, as he strained to sit her wobbly body upright, propping her against the wall for stability. "Did that fucker hit you?" he continued savagely, as he looked guardedly down the dark hall, searching for Otis.

Michelle lurched over groggily, bracing herself against the wall as she gasped for air while shaking her head negatively. She wheezed in and out, glancing fearfully around the house as she labored to catch her breath.

"They killed him...they killed...he's dead," she said crazily, as her voice trembled with terror and she pointed toward her father's bedroom a few feet away.

Mika's eyes widened as he gazed at her in shock, impulsively leaping to his feet while he peered around the house cautiously. "Where is Otis?" he muttered in panic, bolting back down the hall toward the front of the house and poking his head outside to survey the area. He briskly slammed the door and locked it and then turned back towards her, as she sat bent over listlessly, mumbling sorrowfully under her breath.

"Where...is...Otis?" questioned Mika once again, while he carefully crept back down the hallway toward her, looking periodically over his shoulder with apprehension.

Michelle let out a traumatized whimper, as she weakly lifted her trembling hand and pointed in the direction of her father's bedroom. Tears streamed from her eyes, as she began to cry uncontrollably, burying her face in her hands.

Mika took in a deep breath, as he slowly began to inch his way down the narrow hall, past her and over to the bedroom. The door was open and a dim light shone through the opening, which lit the hall drearily. As he let out a fretful gasp, he began to push heavily on the door, bulldozing through the blockade of clutter that blocked his entry. As he carefully stepped inside the room, he peered uneasily over at the clotted blood drenching the bed and focusing on Otis's dead body, sprawled on top of the linen.

"Dear God," he mumbled under his breath, as he staggered back out of the room, queasily holding his sweaty palm over his mouth, while he staggered out into the hall to Michelle. He groggily knelt to the floor holding his stomach, as he began to convulse and choke back on vomit, after witnessing the horrific scene.

"We…We gotta…" He said feebly, stumbling over his words as he tried to catch his breath. "We have to get the fuck out of here," he urged with an ashen face, while he stared grimly at her.

He pushed himself up to his feet and went quickly to the front of the house, where he cautiously peeked out of the cracks in the blinds, carefully canvasing the area.

"Get up…we have to go! Now, Michelle," he shouted belligerently over his shoulder, as he glanced back noticing her now curled up in a fetal position moaning, with her eyes blank and glazed over. Mika ran back down to the hall and roughly grabbed hold of her arm and lifted her clumsily up to her feet. She leaned weakly onto his chest and clasped him helplessly around his neck, as her knees began to buckle. Mika dragged her forcefully down the hall, making his way into the living room, where he cleared the empty beer cans and trash away with his foot, as he lay her dangling body down onto the couch.

"I need you to listen to me. I know my father's connections and these men are dangerous, and they are hunting you down! They got Otis, now they're coming for you. You know too much. We need to get you out of here…Now!" Mika exclaimed icily, as he crouched down, looking piercingly into her eyes. "Where are the keys to the truck?" he demanded soberly, standing up and wading through the junk strewn across the room. He made his way to the kitchen, searching on top of the dining table and in every crevice for the keys, as Michelle watched, in an aimless stupor. Her breath quivered, as she breathed shallowly, staring carelessly at him while he rifled through papers and trash, knocking it to the floor as he sifted through the rubbish.

"Stay with me! Where are the keys to the truck? We need to get the hell out of here," he furiously said once again from across the room, as he hunted hysterically for the keys, ripping each drawer out from its hinges as he raked through its contents.

"I'm…scared…" said Michelle softly, as she sluggishly sat up on the couch, gingerly pointing across the room. Her shaky hand guided him to an empty coffee canister, which had been knocked off the table and had rolled across the vinyl flooring into the kitchen. "We always kept a spare key, in there," she said in a raspy tone, while shivering fearfully as she examined the shadows, throughout the murky house.

Mika immediately dove through old newspapers and trash that surrounded the canister, clutching it in his hand as he savagely tore off the plastic lid, pouring out its contents onto the floor. He hastily scooped up the keys, clenching them tightly in his fist, as he surged back into the living room toward Michelle, kneeling in front of her at eye level.

"Money…how much cash do you have? We can't use any debit or credit cards. I don't want to take the chance of them tracking us," he asked solemnly, as he gently placed his steady hand on her jittery shoulder, staring intently into her bloodshot eyes. "I need you to hold it together, sweetie! Did Otis, keep any cash saved up around here?" he continued to ask her, while frantically scanning the room as though on a mission.

Michelle dabbed frivolously at the sporadic tears that flowed from her eyes, as she peered blurry eyed around the ransacked living room. "He sometimes kept a few extra bucks in the coffee can for gas, but that's it…" she whispered timidly, as she continued to look bleakly over the ravaged room.

"Damn it," shouted Mika bitterly, as he pushed to his feet and kicked the empty can callously across the room. Michelle flinched, startled by his aggression as she cowered low and the can banged violently up against the wall.

"Only thing in there, was the damn keys," he said disheartened, strenuously running his hands through his oily hair as he slicked it back and out of his eyes with his sweaty palms.

As Michelle huddled petrified on the edge of the couch, she stared at him for direction. She gazed cautiously, as he paced back and forth through the room, disoriented and mumbling incoherently under his breath as he decided on a plan. It felt as though time had stood still, until the loud gong from the old clock hanging on the wall in the hallway, echoed throughout the house.

Mika paused anxiously, looking tiredly across the room at the time before letting out an exhausted gasp of defeat. "Come on, let's just go. You can't stay here," he pressed impulsively, while scrambling toward the front window and peeking out through a hole in the blinds into the darkness out in front. Michelle, restlessly lurched up from the sofa and shuffled towards him. She gripped onto his arm fearfully, while she continued to wait for his directive.

As she clung to his arm, Mika loosened the tight grip he had on the spare key and calmly turned towards her with his back to the window. He stared down at her compassionately, while he deftly picked her delicate fingers from his arm. He then gently placed the keys, into the palm of her hand and closed her fist over them firmly. Puzzled, she looked down at her jittery hand clenching the keys and she slowly shook her head in confusion, as she glanced back up at him in dismay. Her eyes slowly welled with tears, as she gazed into his eyes while her lip began to quiver. "But...I don't understand... You're coming with me?" she asked wistfully and before he had a chance to respond, lunged impulsively into his arms squeezing him tensely, as she sniffled against his shoulder.

Mika's eyes closed dolefully, as he let out a compassionate sigh. He wrapped his arms tightly around her, while leaning down and resting his chin tenderly on top of her head. He squeezed her passionately, taking in a deep breath as he smelt the floral fragrance of her hair, before gently kissing the crown of her head.

"You need to go now...I will be right behind you, I promise," he said pressingly under his breath, breaking the silence as they stood embracing in each other's arms.

Michelle gradually released her grip on him, as she haltingly pulled away. She wiped the tears from her eyes while she nodded her agreement, as she stood up tall staring gravely up at him. "Where do I go?" she whispered out nimbly, while her eyes locked trustingly with his.

"Get on the highway and don't stop until you reach the state line," he said zealously, while reaching into his front pocket and pulling out the wad of cash, still with him from the Country Club earlier that day. He fumbled nervously through the money, straightening out each of the crinkled-up bills, as he briskly counted them aloud, before placing them into the palm of her hand. "Here is 96 dollars...that should get you enough gas to get out of town and get you a room at a cheap motel. I'll be a few hours behind you," he continued earnestly, while studying her demeanor and making sure she was following along and paying attention.

Michelle listened hesitantly, then sorrowfully nodded, as she stuffed the clump of cash deep into her back pocket and began to pivot toward the door. Unexpectedly, Mika caught hold of her arm spinning her back toward him, as he delicately reached his hand to her chin lifting her head up toward him. He gazed longingly into her heartbroken eyes, admiring her courage and beauty, while he passionately caressed the side of her cheek.

"Look at me...I'll be right behind you, I promise! I must do this. I need to confront my father face to face. This ends here and now," he murmured painfully, as he glared down at the floor while his voice shuddered.

Michelle meekly bowed her head in agreement, as she hesitantly turned back toward the door, unlocking the dead bolt, and squinting anxiously through the peephole. Her jittery hands tensely clutched onto the doorknob, as Mika inched up to the window beside her, pulling the corroded curtain aside. He peered keenly out into the distance, scoping out the desolate area surrounding the truck.

"It's clear...go!" he roared roughly, signaling her to make a run for it while he kept look out. Quickly, she yanked open the door, running outside and down the creaky porch toward the truck as fast as she could. She sprinted fearfully to the driver's side, heaving open the heavy door with her shaky hands, as she sprang impulsively inside. As she tugged the door closed behind her, she nervously fumbled through the keys, hastily starting the truck and she revving the engine. Without delay, she released the emergency brake, slamming her foot on the gas pedal and peeled off wildly down the dirt path and towards the main street.

Mika stared guardedly out of the window, watching her as she swerved down the dusty driveway. The truck skidded out onto the paved road in the distance, then recklessly sped out of sight and toward the highway. He smirked proudly, while wiping off the sweat that beaded his forehead. He let out a sigh of relief and tiredly leaned up against the splintery door, shutting it closed while the dust kicked up from the speeding truck slowly settled in the air.

"Don't ever turn back…" he murmured.

Chapter XXVIII

Mika strolled up and down the eerie hallway in front of Otis's bedroom, trying to muster up the strength to go inside. He nervously stood with his eyes closed in front of the door, mumbling a prayer under his breath, before carefully reaching his arm out and pushing the door. As he haltingly inched the door open, he began to stumble his way back inside through the debris and slowly shuffled over to the bed. Immediately, he gasped for air, gagging at the balmy smell of the decaying body. He covered his nose with his hand, while he held his stomach. Mika quickly bent down and grabbed hold of a wadded-up sheet from the floor, shaking it out as he continued on his way to the mattress. He shook loose the rumpled linen and draped it solemnly over the bloody corpse.

As Mika surveyed the room, he knelt in front of the bed and began to sift through the bullets that were scattered over the floor. He carefully picked up some of the unused bullets, wiping off the dried blood and flesh that was splattered on them, on his pants. He cleaned each bullet, stuffing it into his pocket frantically, while he continued to search the area for the gun.

Mika's knees shook as he slowly stood up from the floor, vigorously pushing the remainder of the bullets into his back pockets. He stared down apprehensively, at the lumpy mound capped with the blood-soaked sheet that hid the disfigured corpse. Hesitantly, he reached out pinching hold of the corner of the sheet, as he slowly lifted it up. He gently tugged the cloth back, revealing Otis's lifeless hand riddled with blue veins, still holding onto the pistol, soaked in blood.

Frantically, he began kicking at the gun, knocking it free from his frozen grip, until it fell freely to the floor. He jerked the sheet back over his decomposing arm, as he bent down and grabbed the soiled handgun. Mika then sprinted restlessly, over the heaps of wreckage back to the door, leaving the chilling room as he made his way back down the dreary hall. He stuffed the barrel of the pistol deep into the front of his pants, while he loosely untucked his shirt and concealed the weapon, before heading outside.

He unlocked the front door and forcefully pushed it open and rushed out from the house, out into pitch-black night towards his car. He lunged for the door handle, flinging it open as he climbed hurriedly inside.

Mika felt down his shirt, running his hands over his lumpy pant pockets, as he searched urgently for his car keys. His heart began to race, wondering over how he had misplaced them, when glancing up at the dashboard he noticed that the keys were still in the ignition, as the car idled.

Relieved, he gradually settled back into his seat with ease, closing his eyes to calm himself as he breathed in deeply, through his chattering teeth. "Keep it together

Mika..." he murmured under his breath, as he slowly opened his eyes. Without delay, he shifted the car into drive and began to speed steadfastly down the gravel road, on route to confront John, once and for all.

Tears flowed from his eyes, as he drove unwaveringly down the street, reflecting on the horrific scene of Otis's massacred body. Images replayed over and over his head, as he weaved savagely in and out of traffic, pounding furiously on the steering wheel in anger. The thought of Isaac's cold and disfigured body, lying cold in a desolate room, dominated his thoughts as rage boiled his blood and adrenaline pulsated through him.

The tires noisily screeched, as he veered violently into the driveway of his house, skidding uncontrollably to a coarse stop inches away from the garage. He jerked the car into park and harshly rammed his shoulder against the door, bursting it open and falling clumsily out onto the ground. Mika picked himself up off the pavement, stumbling madly up the brick path leading to the front of the house, murmuring incoherently under his breath. He brashly pulled out the gun lodged in his pants, while he staggered purposefully up to the door with hate in his eyes. Mika dug deep in his back pocket for the bullets, carelessly dropping some onto the ground, as his slippery fingers held onto a few of the bloody cartridges.

His knees trembled, as he stood in front of his house, forcibly stuffing the bullets one by one into the barrel. Rounds fell to the floor, as his clammy hands trembled while he loaded the pistol. Mika's heart pounded rapidly, beating out of his chest as he held tensely onto the loaded gun. He pressed his ear firmly up against the front door, listening carefully for any movement on the other side of the door. Mika inhaled deeply and held his breath while he silently listened for any sounds, before gasping for air in defeat. Quickly, he mustered together all his energy and without delay, ruthlessly kicked in the door breaking it open and ripping it off from its hinges.

He stormed fearlessly inside into the entryway, looking around the living room for his father, with only the moonlight that peeked in from behind guiding him. As he gripped the gun securely in his hand, he cautiously made his way slowly across the center of the room and toward the staircase.

"Where the fuck are you, you sick and twisted bastard?" he roared violently, as his voice stuttered from the adrenaline rushing through his veins. Mika paused, while he quietly listened for a response, inching his way closer across the room until reaching his father's office. He pounded violently against the door, thrusting it open with the gun clutched in his hand, as he warily peeked inside, scanning over the dark shadows for John.

As he slowly pivoted toward the stairwell, planting his foot firmly onto the first step, he heard a faint creak coming from the lounge chair behind in the living room.

"Lower that gun, boy," meagerly grunted John with a raspy voice, as he sat motionless in the recliner, hidden in the shadows of the unlit room.

Mika quickly turned around with the pistol raised in the air, as he glared watchfully over at his father's silhouette in the distance. The chair let out an eerie squeal, as John gradually rotated himself in the chair, until he faced him.

They stared soberly at one another from across the dark room, as Mika carefully pointed the barrel of the gun at his head, while his hands trembled nervously. The recliner squeaked grimly as John slowly rocked forward in his chair, reaching for the lamp that rested on the coffee table in front of him. He calmly twisted the knob and the light came on, brightening up the room as he relaxed back into his chair with ease, staring across the room into Mika's teary eyes.

"What the hell have you done?" shouted Mika furiously, as his voice tensely cracked, while tears streamed down the side of his face. He took one of his fidgety hands off the gun, wiping away at the flow of tears that blurred his vision, before quickly placing it back on the quavering pistol, as he continued to aim it at his father's head.

"Come on Mika, what are you doing right now? You going to shoot me? The mayor of this fine city, your father?... Put the gun down," reasoned John condescendingly, as he shook his head doubtfully. "You're no killer...you're too weak," he continued arrogantly, while he glared sharply across the room, piercing him with a riveting gaze.

Mika swayed side to side, appalled by his callous comments, before planting his feet firmly back onto the carpet to reposition himself. He took in a deep breath, as he stood in an unyielding stance, then delicately reached his thumb up, pulling back on the hammer and cocking the pistol as he focused on his aim. "You killed my brother you son of a bitch," he painstakingly shouted in rage, as his hoarse voice screeched, while he struggled to control the gun tightly clutched in his grip.

"I killed Isaac? I…killed Isaac? The piece of shit, was a walking time bomb. I did him a favor…I did all of us, a fucking favor," John lashed out disdainfully, while sharply adjusting the collar on his shirt, loosening the button as he always did when backed into a corner. "How do you think we pay for this stuff, huh? How do you think I've remained in office all these fucking years, to pay for this?" He continued to rattle out aggressively, as his bitter voice grew increasingly louder. "The strings I pulled, to get you into that Ivy League school you wanted and are so proud of. How do you think, these things were made possible? The bullshit taxpayer's salary they give me? You gotta be shitting me Mika… I know, I didn't raise you to be this stupid," he continued to viciously taunt him, while he gradually leaned forward in his chair.

John, cautiously propped himself up from the recliner and slowly began to inch his way away from the chair, as he guardedly threw his hands up in the air, signaling his surrender. He calmly began to shuffle tentatively across the room, towards his office, as Mika vigilantly kept the gun directed on him, while he watched as he slipped past.

"You know son…you were next in line, for it all. I educated you, I groomed you and I trusted you… All you had to do was leave well enough alone, but you were too stupid and stuck on that bitch, just like your brother…and you fucked everything up," he said sourly in a patronizing tone, while he ground his teeth scathingly, followed by a harsh and vile snicker under his breath.

Mika listened, as he kept a wary eye on his father, watching him while he dauntlessly drifted into his office, flicking on the light switch on his way to his desk. He casually moved over to his chair, pulling it out and easing down comfortably into his seat, while Mika slowly followed behind, keeping him at gunpoint.

"Mom, in on this too?" he coldly questioned, while he grimly stared down at him, as John lounged comfortably back into his chair, with a malicious smile plastered over his face.

John paused momentarily, before lunging forward in his chair and reaching across his desk for a framed portrait of the family, they took years before. He gently clasped hold of the photo, studying it as he eased back, relaxing into his chair once again.

"This was a fun day, huh... Where was this, Maui I think?" he complacently muttered, avoiding Mika's question, as he grinned quietly to himself reminiscing the memory.

Mika savagely pointed the barrel of the gun at the wall beside John, who remained focused on the picture. Without a pause, he placed his finger on the trigger, pulling it back. A thundering shot rang out through the room, as the gun discharged a round into the wall, inches from his head. John cowered in shock, as the sound of the bullet ricocheting off the sidewall, buzzed in their ears as it echoed throughout the small room.

"Was Mom in on this too...?" dangerously gritted out Mika once more, as his eyes glazed over icily and the tone dropped to an unnerving chill.

John guardedly adjusted himself, as he slowly sat upright in his chair, vigilantly setting the photo back down on his desk, while he glared up at the handgun pointed directly at his forehead. "Was your mother in on the well-being and continuance of our wealth and…and…and of our legacy? You damn right, she was," he responded brashly, while casually cracking his knuckles, not bothered by his precarious position.

"You sick son of a bitch! You're not going to get away with this," shrieked Mika fiercely, while his hands furiously trembled in anger. He slowly pulled back on the hammer, cocking the pistol once again, as he charged toward the front of the desk, wavering with each step as he panted for air.

John grinned viciously from side to side, as he raised his hands sarcastically into the air, signaling his surrender. Carefully he reached his arm out across the desk for the base of his phone, tugging it close to him, while he studied Mika's demeanor. He smirked caustically, as he lifted the receiver off from its base, leisurely punching in a familiar set of digits as he carelessly dialed the phone.

"Well, before you kill me or have me arrested…there is someone, that I think would like to speak with you," he sneered maliciously, as he finished dialing the numbers on the key pad. He gently set the head set down on the desk, as he switched on the speakerphone.

Mika faltered tensely side to side, as his body recklessly swayed while he aimed the gun inadvertently his father. He leaned curiously towards the phone. He listened attentively, as the ringing on the other end of the phone blared repeatedly, echoing throughout the small office. His knees buckled slightly while his grip on the gun loosened, as he moved closer absent-mindedly to the speakerphone. Within seconds, the sound of a strange man's gruff voice picked up the call, answering the phone in a manner that indicated that the call was expected.

"Come on over here, pretty lady, you got someone who wants to say bye to ya!" griped the husky voice, followed by an eruption of commotion and muffled clatter.

Mika's heart dropped to his stomach, while the air went out from his lungs and his breath turned shallow. He inched closer to the phone, bowing down, as he strained to make out any familiar sounds or voices from the other end of the line.

As he listened in panic, the stifled sounds of a ruthless struggle between the man with the frigid voice and an unknown woman, resounded throughout the room. Aimless shrieks of pain and calls for help broke out between the two, suppressed by the muffled fumbling of the phone.

Mika's legs quivered while he helplessly stood in shock, listening to the flurry and outcry unfolding, as screams and shattering of glass echoed over and over. Tears welled in his eyes as he identified the woman's voice on the other end of the phone, pleading for help, in harrowing and blood curdling agony.

"Michelle...!" screeched Mika with a heart-rending cry, as he fell painfully to his knees with blurred vision from the burning tears in his eyes. Torturous moans bellowed over the speaker, followed by the mumbling sound of impaired babbling, as she struggled to respond.

"Michelle can't come to the phone right now," mocked the chilling voice on the other end, followed by a few more seconds of scuffling. Then the loud and boisterous sound of a single shot gun discharging. Immediately, the call dropped and the phone went silent and the dial tone abruptly blared out filling the void.

Mika felt lightheaded and collapsed to the floor, dropping the pistol as his arms went limp. He curled up on the floor and began to sob heavily in front of the desk, as John let out a piteous sigh while he sat up in his chair, peering over the front of his desk down at him. John glared down stoically as he watched Mika weep uncontrollably, coiled on the carpet pathetic and defenseless.

John calmly picked up the phone receiver, placing it back onto its base to mute the sound. He gradually pulled himself up from his chair, adjusting his collar as he smoothed out the wrinkles on his shirt and began to walk composedly around his desk. He stood coldly over Mika, watching in disgust as he sprawled out moaning, and wailing with desperation.

"Pl... Please, I... I don't know what's going on. I...I'm so scared. I'm sorry," blubbered Mika, in between gasps for air, as he squinted up at his father, with snot and tears streaming down his face. He tugged timidly on his pants leg, as saliva strung sloppily from his lips while he cried out beseechingly. "Please...I don't...I don't want to die..." he continued to plead inaudibly, as his body rocked grievingly.

"Shhhhhh...Shhhhhhh, I know, I know," John replied sedately, as he gazed down at him sorrowfully, then began to run his hands through his curly hair, patting him on top of his head, like he was a stray dog.

John hiked up his pants and slowly crouched down beside Mika, wrapping his arm around his shoulder as he squeezed him tightly and consoling him, while he begged feebly for mercy. He hunched forward, kissing him softly on the top of his head. He deftly rocked Mika, as he wept weakly in his arms.

"It's going to be okay son... It's all going to be okay," he muttered softly in an assuring tone, at the same time he covertly reached for the pistol laying unnoticed on the floor near them.

"Shhhhh...now, now...it's all going to be okay," he continued to reassure, softly whispering in Mika's ear, while he hummed tranquilly under his breath, as he swayed back and forth with him firmly held in his grasp. John discreetly latched onto the gun and plucked it up off the floor, as he soundlessly placed his index finger over the trigger. He continued to sooth and console Mika, rocking him in his arms while he blubbered incoherently, soaking Johns dress shirt with his tears.

John bent down and kissed him on top of the head once more, just as he released his grip on his shoulder, slowly stopping the rocking as he pushed himself up to his feet. He concealed the pistol behind his back, as he stared sinfully down at him, while Mika lay paralyzed on the floor. A single tear rolled down from the corner of John's eye, as he silently pulled his hand out from behind is back and pointed the barrel of the pistol, down at the base of Mika's head, while he was unaware of what was happening and lay weakly on the floor. He inhaled a deep breath as he closed eyes tightly and without any delay, gently pulled back on the trigger letting off an ear-piercing sound, into the top of Mika's skull.

As Mika's body went still and limp, the gun dropped to the floor. John anxiously kicked it away from him, as he gasped for air. Remorsefully, he began to whimper under his breath. He quickly knelt down to the floor near Mika's body, scooping him back up into his arms. He began to hum under his breath, as he resumed rocking Mika's lifeless corpse, swaying back and forth as a pool of blood formed around them. "It's all okay now…" grievously mumbled John, as he leaned down kissing his gory body, once more on the head.

Just then, the office phone began to ring, breaking the silence as the sound pulsated loudly throughout the room. John gazed hazily up at the phone on his desk and hooking the cord with his foot, tugged the base down to the floor where he sat. Without releasing his grip on Mika's body, he leaned over and grabbed hold of the receiver and slowly brought it to his ear.

"Hello…" he answered gloomily, still grief-stricken and in shock over what he'd just done.

"Yes, Michelle you did well! The jobs done now…"

The End